MW01124127

MY MOM AND YOUR DAD

MY MOM AND YOUR DAD

By Leslie Tonner

PANDA BOOKS   ★   Austin, Texas

THOMPSON-SAWYER
PUBLIC LIBRARY
QUANAH, TEXAS

FIRST EDITION

Copyright © 1989
By Leslie Tonner

Published in the United States of America
By Panda Books
An Imprint of Eakin Publications, Inc.
P.O. Drawer 90159   ★   Austin, TX 78709-0159

ALL RIGHTS RESERVED. No part of this book may be repro-
duced in any form without written permission from the pub-
lisher, except for brief passages included in a review appearing
in a newspaper or magazine.

ISBN 0-89015-720-0

*This book is dedicated, with love,
to Emily Curtis,
who knows all the reasons why*

CHAPTER ONE

THE VERY FIRST THING PHILIP THOUGHT OF WHEN HE WOKE UP
was that he was going to throw up.

Then he thought about why. This was the morning he
had to start classes at Edison.

He could hear his mother's voice, all reasonable, saying, "Why should you be nervous? You were admitted because you did so well on their placement test. You *belong*
there."

Ha! As if anyone could tell him where he belonged.
He belonged at Paley. He'd been going to school at Paley
since kindergarten. They knew him there. They liked him
there. He did really well there. Only trouble was, there
was no more *there*. Paley went up to eighth grade, and no
further. He had graduated. He was out.

Maybe if he went into the bathroom he could splash
some water on his face and this terrible rushing of blood
to his cheeks and head would stop. Thud, thud — he
could hear the sound of the blood pumping, for crying out
loud.

Why Edison? Why did he have to go to some elitist,
specially selected place? Why not just another regular
school, like Paley? He was no genius. This was all a joke.

His father's voice would be harsher, sterner, full of
all those "I expects," ready to shatter if crossed. "Philip, I

1

won't hear anything more about schools. You've been accepted and you're going."

"But —"

"No buts. Your chances of being accepted into an Ivy League college will be greatly helped by your admission. You will be among the creme de la creme."

Then why didn't you go there? Philip had wanted to say. But he couldn't. He did not have the power to answer his father. After all, the man might have a heart attack if he did. He made himself take that thought back. What would they do without his father, Jason R. Porter, Esquire, fabulous attorney, ace squash player and workaholic. He wondered how much you could miss someone you didn't see that much of.

"Phil," came the call, distant, a little melodic. Mom.

"I'm up," he called, throwing back the blankets and untangling the sheet from around his legs. This was it. He was moving. He wasn't dead. He was going to have to go to school.

He grabbed his robe and stuck his head outside his door. The bathroom door was closed, light gleaming from under the bottom. Claire was up ahead of him. Primping. Wiggling around and doing all that bathroom stuff that made him late. He walked across the hall and slammed his hand on the door, three times. Boom, boom, boom. "All right," he yelled. "You're under arrest. Come out with your hands up."

The drone of the hair dryer continued. He banged again, this time with his fist. The door opened a crack. "Go to hell," Claire said. The door slammed shut.

The worst part of it was that she was older, smarter, and more popular than Philip, and she didn't have to study as hard. Of course, no Edison for her. She went to Patterson, the snobbiest, toughest girls' school in the city. And she was going to go, no doubt about it folks, to Yale or Princeton. Yup, they were going to beat the door down rushing to accept her. At least, according to his father, his mother, all their relatives, and Patterson's guidance counselor they were. Boy, would she be screwed up if she didn't get in.

2

"Hey, ugly, would you give me a break?"

The door opened and Claire, her beautiful reddish hair now falling gracefully over her shoulders, stuck her tongue out at him. "Baby bro, you've got five minutes. Then I gotta get back in. Is that a pimple on your nose?" she said sweetly.

He closed the bathroom door and leaned toward the mirror, still foggy from Claire's shower. Was that a red spot beginning to bloom? Now he really would throw up. He wasn't going to go to school. He would stay home. He would attend the local public high school. He'd make them send him to boarding school.

Boarding school? He must be out of his mind.

———————————

Claire was already sitting at the dining room table, innocently buttering her English muffin, when Philip appeared in the doorway. "What's that you have on your nose?" Claire said, glancing up. "Is that my cover stick?"

How did she know? Boy, if she could get into Yale for ESP about her personal property she was *in*, man, no doubt about it.

"Good morning, dear," said his mother. She was wearing a t-shirt that said I GOT MY JOB THROUGH *THE NEW YORK TIMES* and a pair of white pants. With her red hair pulled back she looked clean and young. He could never get over how young she looked and acted, compared to his father. People always thought his mom and Claire were sisters. But, strangely, his mother minded that. She liked being a mother, she'd say, and then she'd throw back her head and laugh her kind of throaty laugh. His mom was really neat, for a mother.

His father made up for that, though, by being like a father. His "good morning" came, as usual, from behind his *Wall Street Journal*, which was hiding his cup of black coffee and his Special K breakfast, like they showed in the ads. His father watched his weight really carefully. It didn't do, he would say, in his line of work to give the

3

appearance of being sloppy. His father was in arbitrage. Philip had absolutely no idea what this meant, even though it had been explained to him about a hundred and fifty times. He could understand really tough problems in calculus and he'd gotten an A in physics, one of only seven in his whole class, but he couldn't get what his father did for a living. Maybe he didn't want to know. That was it. Maybe he didn't want to let on he was interested, considering the fact that his father wasn't much interested in him.

It was too bad that Philip didn't look like his mom, as Claire did. He didn't exactly look like his father, either. He was what his mother sometimes called a "mix," which made him sound like a mutt from the ASPCA or something. He had dark, wiry hair, which shot out in different directions if he slept on it funny, and a big, goofy grin. His teeth kind of stuck out even though he'd had braces when he was twelve. But thank goodness he didn't have to wear glasses like Claire did, though she had gotten contact lenses last year. He knew girls said he was "cute" but he had come to understand that they meant that kind of like he was an outfit in a store. Cute wasn't nearly as good as being "terrific" or "adorable." He heard plenty of that stuff from Claire and all her friends. He always eavesdropped on her dates with girlfriends, putting his head next to his bedroom wall. They always sounded so stupid. He could never understand how all those girls "ran the school," as his mother had said. The yearbook editor, the newspaper editor, the class president, the student council president (Claire). What a bunch of jerks!

"Aren't you going to have any breakfast?" his mother asked.

His father turned a page of the paper.

"I'm thinking of dropping Latin this year," Claire said.

"Why would you want to do a thing like that?" his father said from behind his *Wall Street Journal*. It was so weird how his father managed to read and eat and hear everything at the table. But Claire always carried on these

4

conversations with him, even when he was working at his desk in his study, with the door closed. She always went on in. And he listened to her. If Philip did that, he was shooed away: "Not now, I'm busy. Later." He'd stopped trying.

"I'm taking too many courses as is, and I was thinking of electing creative writing."

His father lowered the newspaper. "No," he said.

"What do you mean? It would be extremely useful for me, writing essays, compositions, examinations. My writing could use improvement. You've always told me that."

"It's a waste of time. Continue your Latin," he said, raising the paper. "Besides," came his voice, "you are a splendid Latin scholar."

Following in his sister's footsteps was going to be a big drag, Philip could see that. He knew *he* was supposed to be the Splendid Science Student. Only he didn't really like science all that much. Oh, it was all right. It just wasn't what he wanted to do with his life. He didn't know what he wanted to do with his life. He just knew he didn't want to go into arbitrage.

"Time to go," his mother said all at once, taking a quick gulp of her coffee as she glanced at her brightly colored Swatch.

The sick feeling came on full force and Philip felt dizzy as he stood up, pushing away his barely eaten English muffin.

"Phil, I'm talking to you," his mother said.

"What?"

"Are you going to buy your lunch in the cafeteria? Did you want to fix something here?"

"Aw, I don't know. I'll see what the rest of the kids do. First day, nobody brings anything with them."

"Don't you listen to anybody?" Claire said solemnly. "They don't eat in that school. They dissect bodies during their free periods."

"Whadja say about periods, Claire?" he shot back.

"That will be enough," his father's voice came from behind the paper.

5

"Kiss your father goodbye," his mother instructed.

Claire moved behind her father's chair and gave him a hug and kiss. Philip stood next to her, uncertain as to what he should do. He didn't actually kiss his father anymore. He reached down with his hand, so his father could shake it. But his father stood, suddenly, towering over Philip in his conservative gray business suit, smelling from some kind of funny lime shaving lotion that he favored. He looked somber and distant and big. "Son," he began. He reached out and put his hands on Philip's shoulders. "Good luck at your new school."

Philip nodded.

His father turned around and sat down again.

That was it? He looked at his mother, who had her hands clasped together, expectantly. Did she want more? What did she think was going to happen? The expression on her face reminded him of a picture in his pediatrician's office, a painting called "The Sick Child," in which a feverish little girl lay in bed while a kindly physician held a stethoscope to her chest. The parents, huddled together, watched, and the mother in the painting always made him think of his mom. She was always so involved. So concerned. So worried for him. He wished she wouldn't worry so much, but at the same time it made him glad. He was glad she cared. He didn't want her to suffer on his account, that's all. "It's okay, Mom," he said as he gave her a hug.

She kissed his hair near his ear, then smoothed it with her hand. "Be good," she said.

He took his knapsack from the hall table and let himself out the front door, eager to get away before Claire. He didn't think he could stand her dumping on him this morning. And after his period crack he doubted she'd let him have the last word.

The elevator door opened and he had the strangest feeling that it was like stepping into a time machine that was going to transport him to some different world where he wouldn't recognize anything. *Stupid,* he told himself, but he shut his eyes and crossed his fingers all the same, wishing for a friend, just one friend, right away.

6

CHAPTER TWO

HE'D SEEN EDISON BEFORE — THE NEW KIDS HAD TOURED IT THE past winter — but today it looked different. Bigger, uglier, more imposing, strange. How could you get to know your way around a place this crowded? Suppose he had to get from one end of the building to the other to make a class? He'd never be on time. He'd get detention for being late. They would hate him. He would flunk out.

Edison was not modern and clean like Paley had been. It was dank and smelled of gym lockers and formaldehyde and student sweat. The floors seemed to sag in the middle from the weight of all the years of learning and all the books and desks and heavy brains that had occupied them. This was no ordinary school, after all. This was the school that won the science fairs and the prizes and the college scholarships and the recognition and how could anyone hope to follow in those hallowed footsteps? The kids swarming around were expected to be the future doctors, lawyers, scientists, inventors, billionaires, leaders. What could anyone ordinary hope to do in a place like this? How did he ever get himself into this mess, anyway? All he'd had to do was screw up the admissions test. Only thing was, he'd thought he had. It wasn't just a matter of answering wrong. He was certain he'd done badly even though he was trying his best. He'd figured everyone

7

taking the test must have known more than he did. What a joke to find out they didn't! Yeah, the joke was on him.

He looked at the faces around him, older students eyeing the new ones, looking for cute girls, no doubt. They didn't care about the boys coming in — no competition there. The new students all had the same scared, rabbity look. You could see it in their eyes, big and bulging. Maybe he wasn't the only one who felt he didn't belong. Some people came with groups of friends, from bigger schools, he guessed, where a half dozen or more were admitted. Not like Paley, which was comparatively tiny and from which only Philip was selected from the four who took the test.

"'Scuse me," he heard as an elbow poked him in the back. He turned around and discovered it belonged to the tallest young person he'd ever seen, a scarecrow with a shock of straight light brown hair falling in his eyes, a gangly kid who must have been 6'4 or 6'5 at least. "Hi," the scarecrow said. "Gareth."

"Gareth?" Philip said idiotically. He knew he was staring. All the clichés in the world about tall people came to mind. How's the weather up there? Do you play basketball? Must be a real asset at the Thanksgiving Day Parade. Hiya, shorty.

"Gareth Daniels." A bony hand shot out from an absurdly narrow wrist. Philip shook the hand. He introduced himself.

"Where are you from?" he asked Philip. "What school?"

"Paley."

Gareth's face showed he'd never heard of it. This meant Gareth was probably from Brooklyn or Queens or somewhere outside the city. "It doesn't mean a thing that I don't know," Gareth said. "I've been away at school for so long."

"Away?" Philip said. He didn't know anyone who went away before ninth grade, even though he knew some kids went to boarding schools practically forever.

"Yeah, I've spent the last three years at this experi-

8

mental school community in Vermont. We did school stuff plus a lot of farming and everything."

This sounded really interesting to Philip and he would have liked to know more, but just then a bell rang and everyone began to move very quickly and scatter into various classroom doors. He checked his printed schedule even though he'd memorized it on the way to school, found his homeroom number, and turned to say goodbye to Gareth. But Gareth was gone.

Throughout that long, hot, sometimes tedious and sometimes terrifying first day, Philip looked for Gareth, which wasn't hard to do since Gareth would stick out in any crowd. He did not meet anyone who'd been particularly friendly and he'd kind of hoped he could use Gareth as a starting point. But, unluckily, they didn't seem to share any classes. Until gym. There, sitting folded up on the floor, his arms and legs collapsed like a pile of long sticks, was Gareth. He grinned and waved to Philip, who walked over and sat down next to him. "Greetings," said Gareth. "So we meet again." Philip knew they would be friends because gym was a good place to talk.

And talk they did. Philip found out more about Gareth's school, in between hearing about electives, physical testing, intramural teams, and the relationship of mind to body. The gym teachers apparently realized that most kids didn't care two hoots about sports, preferring to spend their time cracking the books, so they had this whole speech about how you couldn't get maximum use out of your brain cells without enough oxygen. Philip noticed a lot of kids reading, or writing notes to themselves, or solving mathematical problems while the gym guys spoke. He himself liked PE and looked forward to exertion and sweat. Besides, he was good at it and had always made a lot of friends that way. He could see that here it was going to be different. The math team obviously got more attention than the soccer team.

When they left gym, they had one period left in the day — English on Philip's schedule, French on Gareth's. Their classrooms were near each other so they navigated the halls together.

9

"Well, I guess I'll see you around tomorrow," Philip said.

"At lunch?" said Gareth.

"Sure," Philip replied. He was glad he'd have someone to eat with. And Gareth attracted a lot of attention. Philip knew, from experience, that they would soon have a whole group of people around them. They'd start their own circle of friends.

At the door to his English class, a really wonderful-looking girl with long, dark hair tumbling over her shoulders threw her arms around Gareth's neck, bending him over nearly double, hugging him hard. "Liz," he said. "You made it!"

"Boy, just barely," she said breathlessly. "The plane landed at three this morning. We were in the house about ten minutes before I had to get up and come to school."

"How was Zambia?"

Zambia? Who was this girl? Gareth's girlfriend?

"Hey, Phil, meet Liz. We went to school together in Vermont."

"Hi, Phil," Liz said warmly. She had the very nicest smile. She was so up-front. And so pretty.

The bell rang. "Gotta go," said Gareth.

"Are you in there?" Liz pointed to the English class. *What luck*, Philip thought, nodding. But maybe she and Gareth were, like, a number.

That thought occupied him through much of what was a very boring class. Shakespeare and Milton. What a first-semester combo. He wanted to look at Liz instead, but she'd taken a seat just to the left of him and slightly behind, so it would seem as if he were staring at her if he kept turning his head. *Be cool*, he told himself. *She's probably got a million guys. And what was this stuff about Zambia? Very mysterious.*

The English teacher droned on and on. Edmund Spenser's *The Faerie Queene, Paradise Lost, Twelfth Night*. Philip got the feeling that even the teacher knew that studying English was not what the kids were at Edison for. He even paused during his recitation and said so.

10

"I understand full well," he addressed the class over his half-glasses, "that you are in the main concerned with computers and advanced calculus and SATs and getting perhaps one decimal point better in your average than the person sitting next to you." Everyone's eyes swiveled to his neighbor.

"But you are required, by the laws of the State of New York, to take this course. And by God you're going to pay as much attention in here as you do in the laboratory."

Maybe Philip could even like this guy. What was his name? It was written on the blackboard. Mr. O'Malley.

The bell rang. Philip stayed in his seat and waited for Liz to pass into view. She walked by his desk, then went straight up to Mr. O'Malley. He hoped she wasn't one of those goody-goodies who liked to kiss up to teachers on the first day. He watched her talking to him, with her long hair swinging behind her, animated, smiling, really natural. She didn't have a lot of junk on her face. She didn't *need* it. Her eyes were shining and her expression was alive. She was not like some of the girls he knew at Paley who thought they were so cool, whose faces always looked the same, mouths turned down, eyes blank. They had monotone voices: "Hey, howryou, didja hear what that jerk said to me it was like he was talking to an idiot or something and last night on MTV I saw the coolest thing around ten didja watch." It all ran together, like jumbled letters jamming up on a broken computer screen. You couldn't read them. You couldn't understand what they were about. He had come to the conclusion that they weren't about anything at all. They were empty. He always imagined going up to them one day and saying, "Hey, the end of the world is coming, Russian missiles are attacking in ten minutes." And they would reply, "Really. Is that cool . . . did you go to the new Tom Cruise last night . . . there was the coolest thing . . ."

Liz had finished her little chat with O'Malley, so Philip got up from his seat and followed her out the door. She was too fast for him, though, and he would have had to chase her down the hall to catch up with her. He didn't want to do that. Not on the first day and all. He watched her hurry away. Maybe she had to meet Gareth, or another boy. She was the kind of girl boys liked, he knew that. She walked purposefully, with quick strides, in her neat blue jeans and pink sweater. He hoped he would get to know her.

It took him five minutes to find the hall with his locker in it and another five to try and open the lock, which was old and not too responsive to his efforts. He used his birthday mixed with his address as combination, but he could tell he was going to have to allow for extra time whenever he needed to get inside. What a pain. It almost ruined what was promising to be an okay start. He might even get to like Edison a little bit if he could be friends with Liz. Aw, no sweat — the lock opened. He would meet Gareth tomorrow for lunch. Then he could find out some more about her.

Meanwhile he had twenty-five pounds of textbooks to take home, three hours, at least, of homework, and a list of school supplies to purchase that would use up most of his expense money for the next three weeks. Even so, he whistled when he left the ugly, old stone structure that housed his new school.

CHAPTER THREE

PHILIP'S ROOM WAS A DISASTER.

Ordinarily, it was not neat. But tonight it was like the *Titanic* when the ship went down. Just about every space was occupied with crumpled paper, the desk was strewn with opened textbooks, spiral notebooks, looseleaf paper, pens, pencils. The computer was on, glowing expectantly as it awaited the next direction, but its owner was collapsed in a heap on the bed, a copy of his English text open on his stomach, his mouth tensed even in sleep. It was 3:00 in the morning.

The door opened and his mother stuck her head in the room. Stepping gingerly across the mass of paper on the floor, she went to the bed and reached out and stroked Philip's hair. Nothing happened. She pulled on his arm, gently. Finally, in exasperation, she leaned over and said, loudly, "Are you asleep?"

He sat up, suddenly, almost hitting his head on the lamp that extended over his bed. "Time?" he mumbled, trying to see his watch.

"After three. Are you still doing homework?"

He nodded and rubbed his eyes. "Told you this wasn't the right school for me."

"It's always like this the first day. When I was in college they assigned us the entire *Iliad* in one lesson. We had to stay up all night. But we never had an assignment as bad as that afterwards. It was as if they were ducking us in cold water, like an initiation."

"Did you finish?"

"Most of it. The funny part was, they didn't test us on it, not really. Just a general quiz." She smiled at the memory. "Then they assigned us the entire *Odyssey*. But I think there was a weekend in between."

"Lucky you." He rubbed his eyes.

"Why don't you just stack your books, put on your pajamas, and call it a night? I can wake you a little earlier if you like."

"It doesn't matter, Mom. I just hope Dad doesn't get on my case about class standings and averages and getting into the right school. I don't think it's going to be like Paley. It's not that easy anymore."

"Your father loves you. He understands about Edison."

"How do you know that?"

Her expression changed. She got that kind of cold, removed look she always had when she talked about his father defensively. "You never give him credit, Philip, but he cares about you more than you'll ever know." She only called him Philip when she was being very serious. "Don't misinterpret things. People's manners are not the only clue as to how they feel."

Philip squirmed. Next thing she'll be telling me that still waters run deep, or some kind of junk like that. Listening to her defending his father always made him crazy. "I'm going to sleep now, Ma."

She stood up. He could tell she wanted to talk more, about how his father really cared. He didn't want to listen. What did it matter if his mother talked about his father caring? What mattered was that his father didn't act like he did. She didn't know what she was talking about. For a smart person, she could be sort of dumb about his dad. But, he guessed, you had to be that way about the person you were married to. It came with the territory. You had to think they were terrific, otherwise you wouldn't be married, would you?

14

He kissed his mother goodnight and made a half-hearted effort to gather up some of the papers. Half of his math assignment baffled him, he'd read only a few pages of the English, he hadn't studied much Spanish (though that was one of his best subjects and he never had to worry there), and the history text they were using was the biggest bore you ever read in your life.

If it wasn't for the possibility that he might see Liz for more than English class tomorrow, he felt like quitting now. He didn't belong at Edison. The strange part was, what was a girl like Liz doing in a school like that?

Drowsy and drooping over his breakfast, Philip was only dimly aware of a change in the atmosphere the next morning. Usually, breakfast was a quick get-it-over-with affair, rarely charged with any energetic discussions between either his parents or himself and his sister. This morning was different, and it marked a change in his sister's normally benign relationship with his father. Now she was the lightning rod for his disappointment. Where did this come from? How'd she go from family Miss Perfect to The Defiant One in just a day? Philip felt like Rip Van Winkle; how long had he been asleep?

"I am *not* jeopardizing my chances at making any Ivy League schools, Dad." Claire said each word very clearly and distinctly, as if their father was hard of hearing or something. "What makes you think that my sole direction in life is necessarily one of the Ivies? There are other choices too."

"We are not getting into that discussion, Claire." His father had put down his newspaper. This was serious. "You have your admissions material, do you not? We have planned our trips and you're getting those interviews blocked in. What more is there to talk about? Except that you are going to continue the Latin . . ."

"Jason, why can't she switch to something else?" Philip could see that his mother wanted to interfere more but she was afraid. The Wrath of Dad might come down on her head too.

"I am not talking to you, Olivia," his father said, his mouth all pinched up. Philip started to push away from the table. Next it might be his turn and God forbid if his dad discovered he hadn't even finished all his homework the first bloody day of school. He'd really be in for it. He tried to look at Claire, give her some support, though he didn't suppose she'd support him if it came down to a dad battle or anything. Claire was staring down at her toast, as if trying to translate something written on it.

"I've been considering Stanford as a possibility, you know," Claire finally said.

"California?" His father's voice began to rise up an octave. Philip was getting out of there.

The swinging doors to the dining room gave their quiet "swoosh" as he exited. Pleased with his escape, he thought about what he'd been hearing. Perfect old Claire was going up against Mr. Brick and Stone. What was going to come out of that? Nothing, he predicted. He'd tried it himself, a few times. They'd gone to the mat over Edison, for instance. No sale. If he got in, he was going. If he didn't get in, his father had a friend on the board of some elite school in upper Manhattan. How had his father been so sure that Philip would make Edison? Just as he was sure that Claire would make Princeton or Yale? Philip hated his father's sureness, hated his unwillingness to admit that maybe, just maybe, life wasn't so simple. Had he ever been fourteen and feeling like a jerk? Or had Jason Porter always had everything he wanted on little silver trays? He wondered how his mother could stand it.

All the way to school, bouncing around in a subway car with no electricity and no air, he tried to picture Claire in rebellion. It wasn't like she was a total prig. She had streaked her hair last year and he knew she snuck cigarettes with her girlfriends, maybe even some pot, he wasn't positive. But Claire had never openly challenged anything or anyone before. She was this amazing mixture of things, popular and smart, a rule-follower and a rule-breaker. He had never understood how she got away with it. He'd be the last person to find out her secrets, that was for sure. She'd never tell Baby Bro. But he wanted to ask her where she got the guts to rise up, now, senior year. After all, Dad had to pay the college bills, right? A little light clicked on in Philip's head. A boy. Maybe it was a boy she wanted to follow somewhere. He'd have to find out more.

School was hardly the disaster he'd predicted, in spite of the fact he wasn't totally prepared. Seems lots of people hadn't gotten it all straight, either. The teachers were cool about it but handed out similarly hard work: calculus, physics, history (so boring). He felt wiped out by lunch and forgot he was supposed to meet Gareth in the cafeteria, until he nearly fell on his ass when he tripped over a pair of phenomenally long legs stuck out in the aisle.

"Hey, Phil! Hey, asshole, over here."

Gareth was waving a long hand, gesturing at the seat next to him, piled high with books, jackets, everyone's stuff. Moving as if in a daze, Philip shoved past the chair Gareth had stretched himself out on and stood by the piled-up belongings. Nobody paid any attention to him.

"Gareth, sorry for interrupting, but where did you want me to sit?" Philip said. He felt like a fool. Gareth stopped chatting with an intense-looking, shaggy guy across the table and swept some of the things off the chair. Philip swiveled around and asked the girl behind him if her stuff was on the chair. She turned her head. It was Liz. His heart started to go a mile a minute and he felt the crowd's roar around him come sweeping up and almost knock him over. She smiled.

"Yeah, sure," she said, removing a jacket and straw bag stuffed with notebooks, letters, and interesting-looking fabric things (scarves? shawls? sweaters? he didn't recognize this woman-paraphernalia).

He sat down. The food on his tray looked gray, as if it was on black-and-white television. Had he ever dreamed of eating? Liz had turned away, back toward a small

17

group of girls who were listening to her telling some kind of animated story. He heard "desert" and "crazy wind storm" and "blistered hands" before he noticed a couple of the girls staring at him as he eavesdropped. He picked up his sandwich and stuffed it into his mouth.

Gareth tapped his arm. "How's it goin'?" he asked with a smile.

Philip looked at Gareth. Gareth smiled. He knows, Philip felt. He knows I've got this gigundo crush on his girlfriend and he's playing with me on purpose. He set it up, fixed it so she'd be in the other chair and I'd be embarrassed. He tried to swallow his ham and cheese. His throat seemed to have closed up for the day. Couldn't swallow. He started to choke. Tears stung his eyes. Heads turned. *Oh, let me die and disappear from this place so I never have to behold these faces again,* Philip prayed. If he had to spit the sandwich out he'd take the next plane to Alaska. He'd never live it down.

Gareth thumped his back and, miraculously, the ham and cheese went down. Heads turned back. The roar resumed its decibel level of choice — loud.

"Not so good," Philip finally replied, his voice squeaking. He took a swallow of orange juice. So much for lunch.

"Somebody told me there's a bunch of grinds in our class who got through the work," the intense-looking boy opposite Gareth observed.

"Sounds like a lot of bull," Gareth said. "I didn't do any of it."

"None?" Philip said through one more mouthful of dry sandwich. He was afraid he would become known as the Weird Guy Who Did Strange Things While Eating.

"I don't believe in homework. All that matters are exams. Never heard of flunking a course 'cause you didn't do homework."

"What about papers?" Philip said. He seemed to be the only person at the entire cafeteria table shocked by this amazing piece of information.

"Fake 'em," Gareth said.

18

"Don't listen to this garbage," Liz said. She turned to face the other end of the table. Philip felt a long strand of her hair touch his arm as she moved her head toward him. He was afraid to look up. He didn't want her to know. Why did it have to be so difficult? Couldn't he just be friends with a girl? "He's practically straight-A all the time. The genius. He just does everything faster than anyone else. And he likes to brag about it. You're full of it, Gar," she said. But she was smiling broadly. Then she lowered her voice. "I was up till two in the morning, and with almost no sleep from traveling I was like a dead person. I don't know how I'm going to manage with all the work they give us. And English, I never got to English."

Philip felt phenomenally better.

"Where'd you travel from?" he said casually. The little hairs on his arms were standing up.

"Africa." She paused. She knew what he was going to ask. So she answered it herself. "He's an anthropologist. We were on a dig. I had a fantastic summer, but we cut the schedule a little close."

What could you say to that? My father's in arbitrage? Then they always want to know what arbitrage is and he couldn't find any way to make it interesting. Sometimes he told people, "My father sells money." But he didn't want to be cute. He wanted to seem worldly, interesting. In spite of Liz's friendliness and apparent warmth, she seemed very sophisticated. She'd been to all these terrific places, and he'd never been farther from home than camp in New Hampshire and some trips to Bermuda. What a wimp he'd seem like to her. Say something smart. Say something cool.

"Her father is a terrific guy," Gareth said. Uh-oh, that meant they knew each other's families. They must be really close, these two. He decided to get up to leave. As he started to rise from his seat, grabbing for his bookbag, Liz reached out a hand and laid it on his arm. Her skin was cool and soft. He shivered, involuntarily.

"Don't go yet," she said. "We have to figure out what to do about the work. Can't ask Gareth, he's not in our

19

league. Want to get together and share some of the assignments?"

Get together? She was asking *him* out? What a piece of luck! He took a deep breath. "Sure, yeah, absolutely. Real soon." He was blabbering. He was nervous.

"Today," she said, as if it were all settled.

"Today," he echoed. This was one of the best things that had ever happened to him. Maybe the best. He was in heaven. "Sure."

"See you outside at three, okay?" She was looking right at him, right into his eyes. She was so pretty. She was the prettiest girl he'd ever seen.

He gulped and nodded, trying to seem casual, as if he got asked over by beautiful girls all the time. He wasn't inexperienced; in fact, he'd had lots of dates. But he'd never been able to get anywhere with this kind of girl before, the kind of girl who turned heads in the halls, whom everyone liked, who was smart and lively and the center of attention. The girls he'd dated were always flattered to have been asked out by him. Was this why he was acting like a dope? Was this how girls felt when "cute" boys paid attention to them? He felt sorry for all those dates he'd given a hard time.

With a wave of her hand, Liz walked off. Gareth stood up, towering over Philip. "What a terrific lady, huh?" he said.

Philip, guilty, started to apologize. "Hey, we're not dating or anything like that, just getting together to do some homework—"

Gareth threw up his hands, comically, and laughed. "Don't explain to me. I'm not her daddy. Just an old chum from way back when. See you in PE?"

Philip nodded. It was all right, then. Just friends. It wasn't what it had seemed. Why was he so worried, so paranoid? He never used to be this way, not at Paley, where he knew his way around. Here he was just another stranger, one of those faceless numbers, nameless bodies, crushed together in the halls. He should never have listened to his father. He should have challenged him. Edison wasn't right for him, not at all.

20

But then, as he made his way toward his next class, Spanish, he realized that without Edison he wouldn't have met Liz. And there'd never be the adventure of seeing her this afternoon to think about, to dream over, to spin into a terrific fantasy. Back at her apartment (brownstone? co-op? rental? Village? Park Avenue? Upper East Side?) they would lock eyes over Milton, then he would kiss her and she would say, "I'm yours."

He laughed out loud as he lowered himself into his desk. The Spanish teacher frowned at him for talking after the bell. He slumped down into his desk chair and opened his Spanish text. *Buenos días,* Liz, he wrote in his notebook. And he spent the rest of his class writing anagrams on as many versions of Elizabeth as he could dream up.

CHAPTER FOUR

"READY?"

Liz's voice startled Philip as he leaned against a stone retaining wall outside Edison's front door. It hadn't been too bad a day, considering the fact he hadn't been well prepared. But the workload wouldn't quit. It felt like even more homework had been assigned, if that was possible. If his father knew he was going to some girl's house after school instead of going home and working, he'd really be in trouble. He could hear his father now: "What do you think this is, some kind of game? Everything counts from now on. It all goes on the record they examine for college." Philip wondered if his father had ever made a mistake in his life, one single misstep. He doubted it.

He and Liz walked along, directionless, it seemed, since he had no idea where they were going. He decided to ask. "Uh, where do you live . . . uh, I mean, your parents," he didn't know why he'd said that. "I mean . . ." his voice trailed off.

She laughed. Was she laughing at him? He was behaving like an ass. "On the West Side," she said. "Near the Museum of Natural History and the Planetarium." She did not continue, or ask him where he lived, but lapsed into a kind of pleasant silence. He didn't feel ignored, just that she was enjoying being outside in the sun after a day in school. She was breathing deeply and

22

evenly as she walked, with real pleasure. Finally, she said, "It's such a change to be here in this nice fall air, after so many weeks in the desert. The heat weighs a great deal, you know. You feel as if you're carrying around a huge pack on your back. Then at night it can get very cold, and after all that heat, you can practically freeze."

"Did they let you help?"

"They?"

"Your folks, your mother and father."

"My mother's dead," she said, but not sadly, just matter-of-factly.

"Oh. Hey, I'm sorry, I didn't mean —"

"She died a long time ago, when I was six. It was just my father and I, in Africa. You know, this is the first time we've been together longer than just a few weeks in so many years. He sent me away to school because he was never around, always traveling, lecturing, teaching, digging. He's made some fantastic discoveries. Then the museum offered him a position and he decided to stay in one place, at least long enough for me to go to a regular high school and live at home." She giggled. "But neither one of us knows how to cook. He makes all these ridiculous things on the stove that he learned to do in the middle of nowhere. All the ingredients are from cans and everything is mixed in one pot. It's so gross."

They descended the stairs to the subway, showed their school passes, and went out onto the platform to wait for the uptown train.

"Sounds really great," Philip said. His voice sounded hollow, amplified by the cavernous station, and his words seemed particularly inane. He wanted to ask her about Gareth. The heck with the father and this Africa stuff! He needed to know if she was available, if he could go out with her. Or maybe he *was* out with her? Maybe this was a *date?*

A train came thundering in, cutting off their conversation and mercifully giving Philip time to think about how he was going to get around to the subject of she and Gareth. They stepped into the subway and before the doors closed, he said, "Have you known Gareth long?"

23

She smiled and nodded. The train moved out of the station. Over the defeaning noise, she said something to him. He couldn't hear her. "What?" he yelled.

She repeated her words. He tried to read her lips. Why had he asked her now? "I can't hear," he shouted.

"Friends," she shrieked in his ear. "We're friends." She smiled. Face reddening, he beamed back at her. It was all okay. Life was going to be beautiful.

Liz's building turned out to be the big one on the corner of Central Park West. It seemed very fancy to Philip, probably fancier than his own apartment house, which was one of those newer, white-brick buildings with ordinary rectangular rooms.

The doorman smiled at Liz. He told her there was a package. She waited a moment and was handed an odd-looking box all taped up and covered with brightly colored stamps. "Another great find, no doubt," she said with some amusement.

The door to the apartment swung open as she turned her key in the lock to reveal a long, dimly lit hall. Philip waited politely for Liz to enter, then swung the door shut behind him. There was an odd smell to the place, so unlike the clean lemon-oil scent of his home. It was the smell of things old, but also the smell of things interesting. Like a used-book shop or an antiques store.

Walking down the hall Philip passed an old-fashioned dining room with huge wooden furniture— an extremely cluttered room that served as a kind of attic, full of boxes and papers, books and trunks— then entered the living room. The furniture was overstuffed, worn, and comfortable-looking. A layer of dust was visible on every surface. It was not unpleasant but, rather, had the untidy look of a place nobody thoroughly cleaned. Liz made no apologies for the disarray, the pillows wrinkled and tossed helter-skelter, the empty glasses and crumpled napkins, the magazines and books piled up on the floor. It

24

looked like a place where there was no mom running around tidying stuff. But Philip wondered why they didn't have a housekeeper. This was obviously an expensive building and the apartment was huge — it went on forever down one hall after another — and people in apartments like this usually had help.

"Be right with you," Liz said. She threw down her bookbag and went down one of the halls, to her room, probably. Philip perched on the arm of the couch, uncertain as to whether to sit there and get comfortable or whether to wait and see what Liz wanted them to do.

Sunlight pierced the blinds lowered over the big windows. Motes of dust streamed up through the light. Philip stood up and walked over to peer out between the slats. The view was astonishing, high up over Central Park. He whistled under his breath. A view like this was worth a mint. But he noticed that the windows were streaked with dirt and that it was difficult to see everything clearly. Anyone else would throw away the blinds and dusty curtains and reveal this fantasy world to the rooms inside. What a weird house this was.

"BRAAAAAAAAAAAAAAAAAAAAAA!"

Philip whirled around and almost knocked over a small table covered with pictures in little frames. What the hell was that? It sounded like an animal in pain, like a cow getting branded.

"BRAAAAAAAAAAAAAAAAAAAAAA!"

Was Liz in trouble? Was something attacking her? This was like a scene in a horror film, or a Stephen King book. Old house, weird stuff, horrible sounds. It was the gateway to hell, it was an unfrozen monster, it was, it was a man? Carrying an animal's head?

A very big man came into the living room, lifted a huge horn to his lips, and made the ear piercing sound again. Then he lowered the horn, extended it toward Philip, and said, "Want to try?"

"Uh, no thanks. I don't think so."

"Makes quite a racket. Had to. Otherwise how would anyone know it was time to go to war? Or to sleep. Or to get up. Just a gift from an old friend, something to remember her by."

Old friend? War? What was this man talking about?

"Who are you?" the man said, examining the horn closely now, holding it up to the light. "Can't see a blessed thing, can I?" he muttered.

"Daddy, did you introduce yourself?" It was Liz. She had combed her hair back and put on an oversized sweatshirt that said DIG WE MUST. "Daddy, be polite. This is my friend from school, Philip."

"Hello, Philip," her father said, still staring at the horn. "I can't for the life of me figure out why they carved this the way it's been done here. Why isn't it shallower? And the figures are so anthropomorphic. Elizabeth, this could be a very interesting fake, you know."

"You're so rude," she said to her father. "Philip, this is my dad, the great absent-minded professor of all time, Kenneth Cooke. With an 'e'."

"Elizabeth, you still haven't answered my question. Is this or is this not the real McCoy or am I the victim of some global leg-pulling?"

"Not now, Daddy. We're going to do homework."

Philip, who had not said one word in about five minutes, could not get over the way this girl talked to her father. It seemed as if he was her friend, or something. Like a person. And her dad didn't mind. He talked the same way to her. Maybe it was because she didn't have her mother there. Still, this was so different from the fathers he knew — especially from his own father. Even Claire would never be like this with their dad.

"C'mon, Phil," Liz said. "Let's get some food, then we'll work." He followed her into the kitchen. It was a huge, old-style room, with an enormous, ugly sink with separate spouts for hot and cold water, a noisy refrigerator, an immense stove, and cabinets with glass fronts. She opened the refrigerator, which made the noise louder, and studied its contents. "Soda okay? Coke? Classic kind?"

"Sure," said Philip.

26

Kenneth Cooke wandered in as Liz popped the tops on two cans of Coke. He had the horn tucked under his arm and he was holding a sheaf of papers. "I didn't get your name, did I?" he said to Philip.

"No, I guess not. You never listen to me, do you?" Liz said impatiently. "It's Philip."

"Philip who?"

"Porter."

"Porter . . . Porter. I once knew a Porter, but I cannot for the life of me remember why. Liz, do you know a Porter?"

"Nope."

"What does your father do?"

"Business," Philip said, deciding to keep this simple. This guy was so strange, who knows what he was going to ask next?

Mr. Cooke shrugged and said to Philip, "The business of business is business. How would you like to see something?"

"Not now, Dad."

"This'll just take a minute, I promise."

"Daddy, I know all about your minutes." But she was smiling tolerantly.

"It's okay, Mr. Cooke," Philip said.

"Call me Ken," he replied. Ken? He was supposed to call somebody's father Ken? What was going on here? "Come see this," he urged.

He grabbed Philip's elbow and started to drag him out of the kitchen. Liz linked her hand onto his other wrist and pulled in the other direction.

"No, you're not going to do this, Dad. This is my friend and we're going to do our homework."

Ken pulled one way and Liz the other. She was real strong, for a girl. Must be all that digging she had done last summer.

Philip felt himself dragged one way, then the other. "Hey," he protested. "Wait a minute, guys." But they weren't listening to him. This was some kind of game with them. What a weird household. All of a sudden, as if on cue, they both dropped his arms.

"I give up," Ken said.

"Right," Liz shot back. "Let's go, Phil."

"But later on, maybe after dinner —"

"Dinner? No, I couldn't," Philip said.

"We'll see," Ken said mysteriously.

"And don't blow that thing anymore," Liz said as she led Philip out of the kitchen. "We're trying to get some work done."

When Philip opened the door to his own apartment, he felt as if he were stepping back inside reality from some other world, like Alice returning from the looking-glass. He could see why Liz was so poised. With that crazy man around you had to learn to handle anything. But Philip really liked Ken. That was the funny thing. He was strange, all right, but very interesting and silly and a lot of fun and serious, all mixed up together, like dinner had been, in one pot. And the funny thing about dinner was that it tasted good, all those cans dumped in together and stirred up. He was going to have to think real hard about what had happened, to try to make some sense out of it.

CHAPTER FIVE

PHILIP'S PARENTS WERE HAVING AN ARGUMENT. HE COULD HEAR them from the hall after he let himself into the apartment. His mother sounded upset, teary but still firm. His father was cold. So what else was new? He didn't want to feel like an eavesdropper, so he walked along the hall slowly but not *too* slowly, and he heard some of their discussion.

"She is old enough to make decisions. She *has* been for the last few years, only you've been too busy to notice!" His mother. Boy, she really had the guts to stand up to his dad. Too bad it never seemed to do any good.

"She is a child, legally a minor, and I will not be dictated to by my children. My father would have had her over his knee by now." Boy, that tone could freeze the leaves on the trees.

"Thank goodness that you are not your father."

"Are you going to drag my parents into this again?"

"How can you be so short-sighted? She's done everything your way for so long, she deserves a chance to break out."

Their voices got less audible. They must have heard him walking past. He did not dare stop and linger. All he needed was for his father to come out of the living room and catch him standing around. Then it would be his turn, and he didn't need any confrontations. He wanted to keep thinking about his evening, wanted that warm

29

glow of discovery to continue inside his guts. Hadn't gotten much homework done, that's true. He and Liz had, instead, exchanged lists of their favorites — favorite new movies, favorite old movies, favorite tapes, favorite groups live, favorite ice cream flavors, favorite books. They'd agreed on a lot and when they didn't they'd had some really good exchanges about why. It was funny: this wasn't the way he'd imagined it would be with a girl. He'd always thought if you felt romantic about someone you wouldn't be able to talk. This was more like having a friend, like a guy. But maybe he felt romantic and she didn't. What a mess that would be. He didn't understand this business of friendship and love. Could you have both? How was he going to find out?

He closed the door to his room. He didn't hear his parents anymore. Maybe they'd resolved their differences. Obviously, they were arguing about his sister. It was certainly a new and different subject for them to hassle over. Usually he was the one they had to battle over. Should he feel relieved, now that Claire was being knocked off her pedestal? He wasn't sure, but he thought he felt kind of neglected. They hadn't even stopped him when he closed the front door and came past the living room. They never even asked why he'd come home so late when he'd said "after dinner," or who these new people were. His folks, especially his mother, had always cared so much about knowing his friends.

He switched on his desk light and opened his math book. He was going to have to stay up at least three hours to get the basic things done. What a way to begin a school year — behind, right from the start. Only three more days until the weekend and then he'd have to lock himself in and study. No choice there.

As he worked on a particularly difficult problem he became aware of a sound on the other side of the bedroom wall. He stopped writing and leaned over his desk. It was muffled crying. Claire crying? That was a change. He tried to go back to his book but the crying continued. Not really loud hysterics, just sobbing. Really female. Proba-

30

bly had her period or something, he thought. But after a few more minutes he couldn't stand it anymore. Raising his fist, he reached out to knock on the wall. Then he hesitated. "Aw, what the hell," he said.

He walked into the hall and went to her door. He tapped gently. "Hey, Claire, you okay?" She didn't answer. He knocked a little louder, trying not to let his parents hear. But their bedroom door was closed. "Claire, it's me."

The sobbing stopped. Then, after a moment, he heard, "Okay."

He opened the door and walked into her room. It was the larger of the two rooms and had an extra window, because it was a corner room. His parents had always promised that when Claire went to college he'd get the bigger room, but he wasn't sure he wanted it anymore. It was so much hers, he was sure he'd never feel comfortable in it. There were her shelves of books and knickknacks, little ceramic figures, tiny stuffed toys, glass paperweights, her collection of matchbook covers in a huge green glass jar, her records and tapes, her collages of favorite movie stars (all oldies, like Jimmy Stewart, Cary Grant, Humphrey Bogart), and her make-up junk scattered across the top of her dresser — enough lipsticks, eye shadows, tubes of red stuff and beige stuff and white stuff to pile on the faces of all her classmates and the entire varsity volleyball team and still have enough left over to go to a thousand school dances. No doubt about it, this was her space. She inhabited it as thoroughly as those dead Egyptian kings who got buried with all their possessions in a pyramid.

Claire looked awful. Her face was swollen, her eyes were red, her hair was poking up in a million directions.

"Wow, you've really been through it. What's going on?" Philip said. "Is it Dad?"

"It's both of them. They're not going to let me even apply to California. They don't understand."

"What? What don't they understand? I never heard anything about this till just now. Why is it so important?"

"You sound just like them," she wailed.

"Sorry, Claw," he said, using his baby nickname for her. "But you have to tell me what's happening."

She wiped her eyes with the back of her hand. "I don't know, I guess it just represents something really vital to me. This summer I started to feel suffocated."

"You? The Great One?"

She nodded. "I've always been such a good girl and I've played by all the rules, and now I've got these college catalogs in front of me and I can see myself there, at Princeton, or Yale, or one of those places, and it's full of people just like me. I don't want to spend another four years of my life locked in with people like me. I want to know what it's like out in the world. You know, you're so lucky you're going to Edison. You have a chance to see a different cross-section of this city. What have I had?" she said, shrugging her shoulders. "Maybe a great education, but it's been basically the same people since I've been in first grade."

"Maybe you'll see it differently when you visit these schools. How can you know for sure?" Philip didn't comment on what she'd said about Edison. She knew he hadn't wanted to go. Maybe she was just being nice.

"I know, believe me, I know."

"But Dad has a point, I mean, about Ivy Leagues and all that. You can get better jobs or better access to law school and med school and everything."

"I'm not talking about careers, I'm talking about me as a person. You sound just like HIM!" She picked up one of her pillows and punched it with all her might.

"I'm probably not the right person for you to talk to."

"Right now, bro, you're all I've got."

"So why California? Don't you know Dad thinks that only airheads live in warm climates?"

"Stanford happens to be absolutely one of the tops."

"What about Mom?"

"What about her?"

"Are you pissed off at her too?"

"She's really been awful about this. She doesn't have the gumption to stand up to him for five seconds. She's

32

always trying to get in favor with him . . . she's such a mouse."

"Hey, I think you're being really cruel."

"Oh, Mommy can do no wrong when it comes to you, little boy. You've always been starry-eyed about her."

"I think I'm going back to do my work, Claire."

"Offended? Well, maybe when your turn comes to make a decision about your future you'll see where it's at in this household. Whatever God says, goes."

Philip stood up. He didn't like anything he was hearing. He felt sorry for Claire, but he thought she was talking out of pure meanness. And he didn't see what all the fuss was about. They didn't want California, so she could pick another place where the kids weren't all Claire-clones. She wasn't going to apply to only Ivies, after all. Even the Great One needed safety schools.

He tried to tell her this. She waved away his advice with her hand. "I've thought that through already. Someday when you want to hear the rest, when you grow up a little, I'll tell you. Meanwhile, sorry I disturbed your homework."

He couldn't help but feel, as he tried to settle back down at his desk, that some important balance had been tipped and that things at home were never going to be the same.

At breakfast his mother made up for her disappearance the previous evening. "So, how was your date last night Philip?"

"Aw, it wasn't a date, Mom. Just to study."

"And dinner. What did Mrs., ah, what did you say their name was?"

"I didn't. It's . . ." he hesitated. What was Liz's last name? He couldn't remember. His head was a total blank. Well, that would teach him to stay up until 3:00 with homework. He was a certifiable zombie.

"Yes, I'm listening."

33

"My friend's name is Liz. Her mom is dead. She lives with her dad, who's a professor and he's with the Museum of Natural History. They live across the street from the museum."

"That's lovely. What did you have for dinner?"

"He made a crazy stew. He's a really interesting guy, Mom," Philip began eagerly. Suddenly, he wanted to tell her all about his wild night, about the strange household and the horn and the odd food and the mismatched dishes and the strange photos they'd looked at, of skulls and bits of pots and sticks and other things that looked like junk but were actually millions and millions of years old.

"Is Claire favoring us with her presence at breakfast?" his father said.

"I think she had to go in early today. Something about a bake sale being set up for student council," his mother said.

"So, how is your new school?" his father asked Philip.

"It's okay. I like the kids."

"And the teachers and curriculum?"

"Seem fine. I met some interesting people last night," he began again.

"I hope you won't spend too many evenings out at the start of school," his father went on, as if he hadn't heard. "You'll have plenty of time to widen your circle of acquaintances once you get going academically."

"I got a B on the first English quiz," he told his father.

"Humph," his father cleared his throat. "You can do better."

"It was really tough," he said.

"What do you say I get us some tickets for the Knicks this year?" his father said. "We could catch a couple of home games."

Philip had heard this one before. It was his father's attempt to be chummy, to be Dad. But mostly they canceled the evenings because his father ended up being out-of-town or something. He glanced at his mother. She had

34

her encouraging face on, the one that said, "Be-nice-to-him-he's-your-father."

"Sure."

His father smiled, lips stretched tight. He never relaxed, Philip realized. Always tense. What a way to live. Maybe that was what Claire didn't want. To go to school with a lot of Dads, a lot of tense kids who only thought about grades and jobs and money. He would let her know that he saw it that way. Maybe the whole family needed some time in the sun. Being airheads might do them all a lot of good.

"Gotta go," he said, realizing it was time for school. "See you later," he said to his mother.

"I'll be home when you get back. Today's my short day." She had a job at some kind of art bookstore that sold prints and expensive volumes and was always getting letters from New Zealand and Rumania and weird places asking for out-of-print things. Philip knew she loved her job, but he thought the place was full of crazies — people who got obsessed about certain editions of books and who argued about bindings and illustrations and stuff. He was polite to her friends at work, but he didn't like to hang around. Besides, the place smelled. Philip's father called the job "Olivia's folly," and always let people know they didn't need the money, she just did it to have "something to do" now that the kids were growing up.

His mother smiled at him, one of her special, just-us-two smiles, the ones he remembered best from when he was little, when they shared everything together. He realized he always took her love for granted. He didn't have to do anything special to earn it, just be. It was a funny feeling, a different kind of responsibility from the one he felt he owed to his father. Maybe it was like that with all kids and their mothers. But his mother never looked at Claire that way. He grinned at her, wishing they could have one of their talks soon, maybe to clear up this business about girls and friendship and love. He could ask her about that. She'd be honest with him. That was the one thing he knew for certain; no matter what, even if she was pressing him to be a certain way for appearance' sake, she was at least honest about it. There wasn't any bullshit between them.

His heart began to pound as he neared the school, closer to Liz, to the possibility of running into her before English class. *Hey,* he told himself, *this ain't friendship that's going on here. This could be . . . love.*

CHAPTER SIX

A FEW WEEKS LATER THE JIG WAS UP.

"You in love or what, man?" Gareth said to him at lunch. They had become fast and famous school buddies, hanging out together in their free time, spending afternoons or weekend time when Philip wasn't hitting the books (Gareth behaved as if he never studied), going to Tower Records, to the Village, to the movies, out for pizza. Philip had learned a lot about Liz just from listening to Gareth's stories about his weird, avant-garde school in Vermont where they'd kept chickens, raised goats, and adopted piglets. It sounded like the 1960s to Philip. Somebody-or-other's hog farm. But it was a real school. They had classes and took exams, it just wasn't "structured" (the word Gareth used). They sat on the lawn under trees for classes and in the winter inside a converted barn.

Philip didn't understand how they'd learned a thing. He pictured Liz and Gareth sprawled in their blue jeans, cradling baby animals in their arms. Maybe the animals even peed on them, or worse, while they were trying to learn American history. The whole picture was like Henry Thoreau and Walden crossed with Norman Rockwell and Old MacDonald. Still, knowing Liz's dad, it made sense. Philip had not met Gareth's parents. They were always "away" on "buying trips" to the Far East. Only Gareth never said what they bought.

"Yeah, man," Gareth said. "You are in love."

Philip reddened, not from embarrassment at being caught but because he'd been a jerk to think anyone wouldn't know, especially the person who'd patiently answered all of his questions about Liz and the days they'd mucked out stalls and milked cows together. Of course Gareth knew. It was like he was their guardian angel or something, having introduced them. Philip was elated and miserable at the same time. Now what?

"I guess so," he said, stuffing the last bite of his cafeteria hot dog into his mouth, trying to stuff down the welter of feelings inside too.

"That's cool. She is a really terrific person. We've been friends since we were eight years old. And her dad too. Did you know he was famous? That he's made all these big discoveries and everything? There've been articles about him in *Natural History* and something in a series on Channel 13 and stuff. He has a whole theory about the route some primitive tribes took that has to do with one of the cradles of civilization. Man, it's too deep for me, but you get him talking about it and wow!"

Philip knew about the talking. He hadn't known about the famous part. All he read was *Sports Illustrated*, and he never watched science on TV. It seemed too much like basic lessons for kids. Liz's dad would eagerly explain something to you for hours, if you let him. His work was so important to him; you could see from the expression on his face as he talked that he entered another world when he described it. As if he was there, living there a billion years ago. Transported, that was the word. Like the Twilight Zone, *ooooo-weeeeee-ooooooo*.

"Not boring, like other parents," Gareth was saying. "Crazy, but not a drag. Liz doesn't listen to half of it, of course. She's heard it all before. But she's good to him, makes sure he eats and things like that. When he sent her away to school she was always collecting fresh vegetables to make a package for her father, out in some desert. Isn't

38

that a riot? He should have been sending food to her, like cookies and candy, but she was wrapping up summer squash and radishes and carrots and putting all these weird stamps on everything. I'd imagine her dad somewhere in the desert opening it up and laughing and then feeding it to the camels.

"He came to school once to give a lecture about his travels and he brought a slide show with him. Some of the slides were in upside down and everything but it was great. After all the laughing everyone began to listen. It must be something to have a father like that."

"Yeah," said Philip. "Not like a father at all." Sometimes, after visiting Liz, he'd had the same thoughts himself. To have this person as your dad — someone interesting, someone funny, someone real. "What's your dad like?"

Gareth stretched his long, long legs out and began to get up from his cafeteria chair. "You don't want to hear about my father. Too dull."

"What does he do?"

Gareth shook his head.

"No, I'm really interested. I'd like to know more." From what he'd seen of Gareth's home, a townhouse in the East 60s, his father must have made a great deal of money.

"Phil, man, I don't know for sure what he does. He calls it imports. I call it sinister. I think he brings bags of money back into this country."

"Money? What do you mean?"

Gareth raised one eyebrow. "You know. Sinister stuff."

Philip could find out no more because the bell rang and the cafeteria rose as one to empty trays, retrieve bookbags, and shuffle toward the exits. "Sinister" had a really bad connotation. Did Gareth mean that what his father did was illegal? He'd never known anyone who was illegal before. Or maybe it was the CIA. Maybe his dad worked for the government in an undercover way and couldn't let anyone know what he did. But what would account for all their money? Gareth's home was filled with fantastic art, abstract paintings that looked expensive, smooth stone sculpture sitting high on pedestals, puffy white couches placed in front of oddly shaped low marble tables. Philip had seen expensive homes before; he'd had some friends at Paley who were the children of famous people, and he knew money when he saw it. But he'd known their parents, at least had met them once or twice. And the source of their wealth was available for all to see, in their latest Broadway show or their latest hit movie or even in their grandparent's fantastic invention (he'd known the grandson of the man who invented some kind of push-button top for spray products).

When he thought of his own father, going to his job every day, earning a lot of money but not tons of money, buried behind his newspapers or his files or his pile of correspondence, he felt like going to sleep. His father was just a businessman, real ordinary, although he acted as if he were some great man half the time. Where was the fun in that? And how could he expect his friends to be interested in such a person? They'd say "Hello, Mr. Porter," and he'd say "Hello" back, and that was the end of it. No weird, adventurous, or humorous stories; no hint of scandal. Just regular, everyday sanity. He didn't understand how his mother put up with it. It must be so boring to be married to such a person. She should have found someone more entertaining.

Meanwhile, though, his boring dad and his long-suffering mom (as it seemed to Philip) were giving his sister Claire an incredibly hard time. California was out. They wouldn't sign the application, and that was that. His mother had knuckled under, his father had won, and Claire was defiant and miserable. Philip suspected there was a lot more to it than just this apparent whim of hers to "find someplace where the kids aren't just like me," but he couldn't find out the truth. Her door was closed to him. What did she want? Was he supposed to influence their dad? Slay the dragon? He knew exactly what his father would say if he tried to approach the subject: "Mind your own business." Finished.

When he asked his mom what had happened, she dismissed his inquiry with a short reply. "Claire is going to compromise," she said.

"But why wouldn't you let her?"

"Your father felt very strongly."

"Would you let me?"

"You are not Claire, Phil."

"Don't rub it in, Ma."

She laughed. "That's not what I meant. A boy of eighteen and a girl of eighteen are not the same people."

"But Mom, Claire is much more responsible than I am."

"I don't think so."

"You don't?" Philip's mouth dropped open in amazement. After years of having Claire held up as a paragon, *the* paragon, this was news. "But she's always done terrifically. She's much more organized than I am, her grades are better — "

"I didn't say organized. I said responsible."

Philip retreated back to his room to think that one over.

Liz's father didn't think that being responsible was important. He told Philip so the next time they were together, which was on a Saturday, following a movie Philip took Liz to see (something in German about a girl during the Second World War who acts as a runner for the Resistance but who falls in love with a German soldier). Philip didn't like the movie very much, so he spent a lot of time in the theater thinking about how things seemed to be turning upside down, with Claire getting all the flack and him looking like the "good" one. He wasn't comfortable with the idea of being good — that was too babyish or girlish — but he liked what his mother said about responsible. That had a solid feel to it. He felt respected.

Liz cried at the end of the movie, which woke Philip

41

out of his reverie. When the lights came up they sat in their seats, then made their way outside to the glaringly bright sunlight pouring over the buildings and the huge structures across the street that made up Lincoln Center.

They sat in the sunlight near the fountain for a while, Liz talking on and on about the great director of the movie, Philip trying to sound intelligent and informed though he hadn't seen many subtitled movies. It wasn't that he had something against foreign stuff; it was more that he didn't know too many people who would go with him. Not his friends from Paley, for sure, which reminded him how little he'd seen his buddies this fall. They'd all drifted apart, to different schools, and their phone calls had become less frequent. Philip saw Gareth and Liz most of the time when he was free. His mother had begun asking him little questions about Liz and wondering if he might want to "bring her around" to their home one day.

They walked back to Liz's building and, once in the apartment, went straight into the kitchen. Liz's dad was seated at the counter, absorbed in a manual that had come with an electric appliance. Near his elbow, on the counter, was a food processor.

"I'll be damned," he said to Philip and Liz when he realized they had come into the kitchen, "if I can figure out how the hell this thing works. What good is a Ph.D., anyhow?"

"Someone got my dad a present. I think it was because he fed them his canned stew," Liz said. "This is supposed to make cooking a snap."

"But what if you don't cook?" her father said plaintively. "It couldn't possibly make a good fried egg."

"My mom has one of these," Philip said. "I'll show you how to do it."

And that was how they got to talking about taking over, being in charge, responsibility (that word again). Liz's father said, "If I had thought responsibility was the be-all and end-all, I'd never have made any of my discoveries. There would be no work in my field. To make a meaningful contribution I had to be irresponsible to some of the people who loved me . . . love me," he said, looking at Liz. She smiled and tossed her head, shaking her long hair. She was always serene and behaved as if she'd heard everything before, so nothing fazed her. Philip was a little in shock. People in his family didn't go around *talking* about love.

"My mother told me I was responsible the other day, for the first time. I guess it's the only time I remember her telling me something about myself to my face."

"Well, young man, you're responsible enough to show me how to use this advanced technological miracle. Now what can we make with it?" Liz opened the refrigerator door. Philip looked in the pantry. They ended up slicing potatoes for french fries. Liz's father kept changing the settings, so the potatoes were a variegated lot, some criss-cross style, some long and slender, some discs, some plump fingers. They fried them up in oil and ate them greedily. Between mouthfuls, they talked. Liz's dad asked Philip about his family.

"So this nice mom of yours, what does she do?"

"She works in an art bookstore that's sort of like a gallery, too, with drawings and prints sometimes. The books aren't all new, lots of them are old. Kind of a musty place."

"You don't like must, I take it," Liz's dad said.

Philip shook his head.

"Yet you put up with us. Amazing, Elizabeth, what tricks the mind can play."

"Stop it, Daddy. Want to go in my room, Philip? We can listen to my new tape," Liz said.

Philip was enjoying the attention he was getting. In fact, whenever he was at her house he got a lot of attention. Not like at his house, where he was lost in the crowd most of the time or just too unimportant to be addressed. His parents didn't ask him how he felt, at least not his dad. His father talked about tickets to opera benefits, the stock market, some new four-star restaurant they were going to take some big client to, or an obscure story in the paper that probably nobody else in the world read, except the guy who wrote it. Philip could remember two or three of these tidbits, one about a new process for freezing some part of the human body (pancreas? spleen? thyroid glands?), and another about some Indian tribe in the Andes that had a collection of rare antique watches. But here, at Liz's house, a swirl of fascinating stories rose up around him whenever he came over, and he was the center of that vortex. It didn't occur to him to wonder if that same vortex rose up around other favored guests. He'd never seen anybody else in the house, except for a shy cat who made rare guest appearances in the bathroom off the kitchen.

"My father can be too strange," Liz said when they reached her room. But she was not apologizing.

"Wait till you meet mine," Philip said.

"Oh, I'd like to. When?"

"I'm not sure . . . I mean, he's real busy, he's never around. I wouldn't know . . ."

"Cut the crap, Phil. You don't *want* me to meet him, right?"

"He's boring."

"Do you have other girlfriends you bring around?" she said with a smile.

"You aren't going to like him."

"Let me be the judge of that. Ask."

"My mother really wants to meet you."

"Really? Why?"

"Because I like you. She wants to know about things I like."

"I'm a thing?"

"Don't get smart. You know what I mean. She once bought a book on soccer when I played on the team at school, to follow the fine points of the game. She likes to know things well. She studies."

"You like her better, don't you?"

"Than what?" He was uneasy with her question.

"Than your dad."

He paused a beat. "Yes."

"No sin, I mean, to like one parent more than another. They don't come in matched sets, you know."

44

"No, dummy, I didn't know. I thought they cloned."

She hit him in the head with her pillow. "Jerk!"

They took a few half-hearted swings at each other with the smaller throw pillows, but Philip felt too full from the french fries to horse around. There was this strange pulling in his chest, and his heart was going like mad. Liz looked at him, her mouth open slightly, her eyes heavy. He knew that she wanted him to kiss her. Would he? Could he? He closed his eyes and made a kind of dive toward what he hoped was her mouth. His lips landed awkwardly on the corner of her mouth but she swung her head slightly toward him. Kissing her was the nicest thing he had done in so long. He wanted to stay there forever, his mouth on hers. She pulled her head away slowly and, sighing, collapsed back against the pillows.

"Now can I meet your parents?" she said.

Sometimes she was just like her father. Weird.

CHAPTER SEVEN

THE DAY THAT LIZ WAS TO MEET HIS PARENTS, A COOL EARLY NO-vember Sunday, was also the day Philip realized he didn't know what was going on in his family anymore.

It used to be that everyone had their assigned roles. His father was, of course, the Fearless Leader, his mother the Sweet and Nice One, Claire the Golden Girl, and he? What was he? Sons were supposed to inherit everything and carry on the family name, but Claire said she'd never change her name, not even if she got married and had children, and she was going to be a great lawyer or busi-nessperson or politician. So what did that leave him? He was like the utility man, always there, sometimes filling in for someone, famous for just being around.

Well, that was then. Now Claire had abdicated her role. Her grades had started to slip, especially in Latin, and she spent all her time in her room writing letters or working on what she called "my novel." Sometimes, judging from what she said about her work, Philip thought she was writing a book about the family, about all of them. He was dying to see what she said but he wouldn't go near her room or her pile of white, typewrit-ten pages that she carried everywhere with her.

Liz said that Claire was changing her focus, that in-stead of identifying with her father (which Liz called Oedipal) she was identifying with her mother (and when

46

she said this, Liz sounded wistful, as if she missed terribly having a mother with whom she could identify).

"I don't know about that Freudian junk, but I do know that you don't have to be a famous shrink to see that my sister is mad at my father and she's going to do anything she can to get back at him, including screwing up her chances to go to Yale. She talks all the time about some writing program in Iowa. They're not letting her apply to California and she's talking about Iowa!"

"At least it's closer than California," Liz said.

"It's like she wants to bury herself somewhere out there, in those cornfields."

"Real dramatic. I'd like to meet her," Liz said.

"She's not your type."

"Why? Because she's your big sister? I always wanted a big sister more than anything. Someone to show me how to do my hair, what to wear, how to act around boys."

"You don't do badly at any of that," Philip said, amazed he had the courage to get the words out but finding it easier to be bantering than he thought. He wanted to kiss her again but they were coming toward the entrance to his building and he didn't want the doorman to see, or any of the little old ladies who always seemed to be hanging around the lobby on nice, sunny days.

"Are you nervous?" he said to her as the elevator moved up toward his floor.

"Nope. Are you?" Her eyes were shining. She was excited. Philip hoped it wasn't because she thought she could learn something about him from meeting his parents. They didn't have anything to do with who he was, not at all. He was his own person.

He rang the bell, as if they were guests, forgetting to use his key. His mother answered the door. She had put on one of her "grown-up" outfits, as Philip defined them, the kind of silky blouse and wool skirt she would wear to a parents' meeting at Paley or to work on a day when she was going out for a special lunch. She had make-up on and some new perfume that smelled nice. She smiled

47

warmly at Liz. "I'm so glad to meet you," she said, extending her hand.

"Hello. I'm Elizabeth Cooke," Liz said, not giving Philip a chance to make an introduction the way he'd been taught to do by his parents.

"Cooke?" his mother said pleasantly. He realized he hadn't told his mother much about Liz and her father; she'd been so preoccupied with the problems involving Claire that her usual interested questions about his friends had, for the time being, been put aside. "Is that like Captain Cook?"

"Captain Hook, Ma," Philip said teasingly. There was something here he couldn't define, something happening. Or maybe it was his imagination. His mother was looking at Liz.

"Cooke. With an 'e'," Liz said.

They were still standing in the foyer. "Let's go inside, Mom," Philip said. The three of them walked toward the living room. "And what does your father do? Philip mentioned some position with the museum."

"My father has received a grant for research and lecturing and has accepted a post at the Museum of Natural History for now. He'll be off again soon, though. Maybe this summer, and then when I go off to college I'm sure he'll go back to Africa for good."

"Africa," said his mother. "What is his name?"

"Kenneth Cooke."

"How interesting," his mother said. "Let me get you some tea. Philip, would you show your friend around the apartment while I get the tray?" Her voice had gone up as she was speaking, like she had something in her throat, and her face was pale under her pink make-up.

"Are you okay, Mom?" Philip said to her quietly, as Liz walked over to look at a collage hung over their fireplace.

"It's nothing, dear. She seems like a very nice girl," his mother said. "I'll only take a few minutes. And I'll send your father in. Where is Claire?"

Philip didn't know. "Probably in her room, writing."

48

His mother shrugged. "I can't be responsible for her behavior these days." But she still seemed preoccupied, thinking of something else.

"You know," Liz said to him as he joined her near the fireplace, "this is really extremely good."

"It is?" Philip had grown up with that collage hanging in his house, first in their smaller apartment ten blocks away, then in his parents' bedroom here for some time, and finally back in the living room. It was his mother's favorite, but he'd never really looked at it before.

Liz was studying it. "Your mother is nice," she said. "You look like her."

Philip shrugged. He wished the day were over and he and Liz were back outside, taking a walk, or in her apartment, with all its strange secrets and art objects that looked like buried junk, spears and skulls and odd-shaped drums.

His father made an appearance, dressed in his Sunday working-at-home clothes: a Ralph Lauren knit shirt, chino pants, and topsiders with no socks. Sometimes Philip thought his father dressed like someone in a *New Yorker* cartoon.

His father was as friendly as could be expected. He, too, was cordial to Liz, interested in hearing her comments on the collage and on how nice the apartment was. He paused a moment over her name too. "Cooke?" But then he moved on to another subject. As usual, he wasn't much interested in what her father did. He didn't think anyone's father was as interesting as he himself was. So he talked a little about his work and what he was hoping to do at Christmas time (taking the family to Dix Bay). Liz nodded and listened and contributed a bit here and there until Philip's mother came back after a while with the tea and little bakery cookies she'd bought. He was touched by her concern with having everything right but thought she was unduly nervous about meeting someone who was, after all, just a friend (his parents didn't know they'd *kissed* or anything).

Claire eventually made an appearance, carrying her

"manuscript" and dressed in her oversized screaming pink t-shirt, legs bare, feet in faded pink fluffy slippers. She nodded at Liz, took three cookies, announced she had to do more work, and left the room. Philip's parents exchanged concerned glances and his father excused himself. Soon they could hear voices raised in another part of the apartment. Liz was sipping her tea and talking about art with his mother when Philip announced that they had to be going.

"Why?" Liz said.

"That movie. Remember the one we were going to see?"

"No," she said. Liz could be so blunt sometimes, so dense. She lacked that phony social grace he saw often in his mother and his sister. Maybe that's what came of not having a mother or a sister. She was as direct as her father.

He tried to signal her with his eyes but she paid no attention. For a long, excruciating five minutes he stared at his hands or fiddled with his teacup (he hated tea) while their conversation continued. His mother was being terribly polite, more than he was accustomed to with his friends — probably because this was a girl and she knew that Liz was important to him. *Planning the nuptials already,* he thought foolishly, then shrugged off the thought. Women. Who knew what they thought, anyway?

Finally, he heard Liz saying, "It's been so nice to meet you, I hope I have a chance to see you again soon," and his mother replied, "Likewise." Likewise? He never *heard* such talk from his own mother. Was she trying to impress this girl? She was acting very strangely for someone usually sensible and direct.

A few moments after they left Philip's apartment, while they waited for the elevator, a front door slammed and around the corridor came Claire. Her hair was a fright and she had on layers of summer clothes, several t-shirts combined in strange colors, and day-glo sneakers. She was going the whole rebellion route. Next Philip expected something awful. Drugs? Pregnancy? His sister wasn't exactly sane anymore.

Claire nodded at them and hummed as they waited for the elevator. Philip wanted to ask her why she thought their mother was behaving so strangely but he didn't want to in front of Liz. The elevator finally arrived and they got on. Claire said, "So you're the famous girl."

"And you're the famous sister," Liz said.

Claire smirked.

"I heard you were the star of your class," Liz continued.

"Used to be."

"So did I," said Liz.

"Don't listen to her, she still is," Philip said.

"He doesn't know anything. We're only in English together," Liz said in a confiding tone.

Claire looked at Liz, then Philip. The elevator door opened. As they stepped out, she said, very casually, "Maybe you want to come with me? I'm meeting some friends downtown. We're going to a bookshop where people can read their own stuff. They dared me to bring my book. It's not finished," she explained to Liz. "But they told me that getting feedback at this stage could be very important."

"Since when were you so big on being a writer?" Philip asked. "It's only a few months ago you even mentioned taking creative writing."

"What would you know? You don't know who I am," said Claire. "You don't and your parents don't."

"Look, you don't have to get hostile." He glanced at Liz, who had certainly seen a lot of family conflict for one day. "Maybe we have something else to do today. I didn't mean to suggest I might have made your acquaintance. After all, we only live in the same house."

"I'd like to go," Liz piped up. "If it's all right with you both, that is."

"Me too," said Philip. He wasn't going to get left behind while his date went out with his sister. All afternoon, this conspiracy of women. He didn't understand it. What he wanted was maybe a walk in the park, some Sedutto ice cream, and maybe a quick visit to Liz's house.

Her father might be around, and they could talk. He enjoyed those conversations a lot.

"Then let's go," said this new Claire, who was a slob and who kept deep secrets and who didn't have the same friends anymore and who was truly like a stranger to him, her own brother. Pretty soon, he figured out, nobody in his family would be talking to each other. If that was how it was going to be, he might as well find himself another family. Like Liz's — where he was appreciated and where they listened to him and took him seriously. Anything but the funny farm his house was turning into.

CHAPTER EIGHT

THE AFTERNOON CONTAINED SHOCK AFTER SHOCK.

The first was Liz's friends and the bookshop. All those giggly high school prisses had disappeared, replaced by a collection of punky-looking females with chopped-off hair dyed strange colors. They each wore two different earrings, some very strange objects like heads of tiny dolls or what looked like nooses of twisted copper (later Liz said they were IUDs). Their clothes were much weirder than what Claire had on, things with holes in them, lots of black, antique stuff like old football jackets with strange patches sewn on. The guys were strange too, with the same awful hair and wild eyes, some with eye make-up on. Philip had never much liked punk styles or punk music, and he felt out-of-place in his neat clothes and straight-looking hair. He saw that Liz, dressed in a pretty skirt and sweater for the meeting with his parents, did not feel odd at all. Must be all those years of getting to know African tribes with her dad at her side that made her comfortable in situations like this. No bushmen or Ubangis or whatever they were could look as weird as a bunch of punks. The question was, how did his normal, once-sane sister stumble onto this group?

They greeted her like an old pal, but she didn't introduce Philip or Liz. There was a great buzz about whether she would read or not, but she gave no indication as to whether she would. The dusty shop, with rickety shelves lining the walls and some folding chairs in the front area near the cash register, was not designed to hold a lot of people. Within the next half hour, as everyone crowded in, the air got hot and pungent with the smell of bodies. Philip wanted desperately to leave but he also wanted Liz to think he was cool and mature. What he did instead of saying, "Let's go," was try to get her to say it. "Are you too warm?" he asked. "Is it too crowded? Are you claustrophobic?" But she was enthralled by the oddness of it all. Why would she be any other way, with a father like hers and a strange, flexible upbringing? And no mother to teach her to be scared of things like this.

After about an hour, while a few people got up and read their poetry, which sounded like just a bunch of words to Philip and not understandable words either, Philip was ready to take Liz by the hand and force her to leave. It was then that Claire got up to read and the shocks began to occur. The first was that she was good, really good, and the second was that she had written about her . . . his . . . *their* family. Including him.

Claire read too softly at first, haltingly, but then gained confidence as she sensed her listeners' involvement growing. Her excerpt or short-story fragment, or whatever it was, concerned a family living in New York City, a mother who was youthful but searching for something more "fulfilling" than marriage or her part-time job (didn't his mother like her job? wasn't the family enough for her?); a father whose attachment to his family stood in the way of making an important business deal (what was that all about?); an older sister who lacked confidence, whose "artistic personality" was being swallowed up by "details, details"; and a younger brother who sailed through the turmoil "not caring about saving anyone's ass but his own." That was what hurt. She saw everything backwards, or maybe that was what writers did when they talked about their own families so no one would know it was really *them*. Unless you were a member of that family, of course.

54

Philip sank lower and lower in his chair as he tried to escape the words issuing in what now resembled a flood of accusations from his sister's mouth. He was positive she had told everyone that her brother was there (even though he'd been invited at the last minute) and they were waiting for her reading to end so they could turn around and sneer at him. But how different was this picture Claire had painted from what went on in his home? True, he saw his parents differently, but that was his prerogative. He thought Claire watched out for her ass only too well; suppose he'd written that into a story? As the crowd in the bookstore applauded her efforts, Philip wondered where Claire had hidden all of this rebellion that had changed his sister's appearance, goals, and perceptions. And if she had slid so far away from the Claire he formerly knew, where did that leave him?

Liz had applauded, too, and she told Philip she was proud. "You never told me your sister wrote. She's very good. Maybe she can get published."

Published? Those things about him, about his family? Did Liz now think he was some kind of jerk? The brother in the story stood by as the sister tried to destroy herself; the mother and father wrung their hands but had nothing to contribute. The punky kids approved. They liked hearing about stupid parents. And stupid brothers.

"C'mon, Liz, let's get out of here." He took her hand and tried to pull her toward the door.

"Could you wait a minute while I congratulate Claire?" She stared at his face. "Is something wrong?"

"No, I just feel hot and sweaty. I'd like to get out of here."

She had a funny look on her face. She'd heard the story; was she embarrassed or did she understand?

"Look, Liz, I want to take you home and then, I don't know. Maybe I'll go for a walk or something."

"It's okay. We can get out of here. Why don't I walk with you for a while?"

They left without seeing Claire. Philip waved to her across the room; she was sitting on the floor clutching her manuscript, her face flushed and her eyes shining. She looked as pretty as he'd ever seen her but also different. Grown-up, he guessed, out of reach.

For a dozen blocks he walked along with Liz, not talking. She respected his silence. They left the strange East Village neighborhood of the bookshop and entered a more conventional area of streets with brownstones and white-brick apartment buildings, sidewalk cafes with a few patrons braving the cool air to catch a last late-autumn touch of sun.

Finally, Liz broke the silence. "Look, I think I know what's bothering you. But you're taking this all wrong. She's not spilling any family secrets. She's using her life to create art. Everybody does it. Painters, writers, composers. She's a good writer. She's got talent."

"So how come I never noticed? Because I was too busy staring at myself in the mirror?"

"That's not what she said. Anyway, what does that character — John was it? — what does he have to do with you?"

"We're both related to the author."

"But the author isn't the narrator of the story. The narrator is the author's creation. You're leaving out the magic."

"What magic? You write about your family the way you see them —"

"No, that's not what I mean. You're talking about a diary. I'm talking about art. She created a family on the page."

"I have to tell you that I don't think what she said was right, not what I've seen."

"Of course not. She just took your family structure and she built her own creation on it."

"Made it up?"

"Not made-up, exactly . . . spun out, probably. Anyway, everyone always writes about their own families first. I did."

"You too?" he groaned.

"Yes. I wrote about my mother and father, what they

would have been like if she had lived. Having arguments, sitting at the dinner table, me coming home after school and saying, 'Hi, Mom, what's for dinner, that's a nice dress, I want you to meet my friend Debbie.' "

"Normal."

"Yes, normal. Normal life. Not living without a mother and going to a crazy school and having your father send you boxes from places in Africa you never heard of with weird animal horns in them and funny twisted bits of bark and rocks and shells and long feathers from birds that don't live anywhere else. Even in my crazy school the kids got boxes with licorice sticks and clear nail polish and teen magazines and pretzels in them. They shared the pretzels. I couldn't exactly share my rocks and shells, unless someone needed a paperweight. So I created this fantasy about having a normal life, and sometimes I'd even talk about my 'mom' from these stories like she was a real person. 'My mom got this great new dress'; 'My mom bugs me a lot about my hair.' But I said these things to people who didn't know me, who didn't realize that she was dead. I never really knew her at all, just the photographs in my father's drawer of me when I was little and she's holding me in her arms. She was very pretty."

Philip felt foolish. Here he was, complaining about someone writing about his family when he had a family and Liz didn't have one, except for her dad. He cleared his throat, which was kind of choked up, and said, "Your dad is really great, though, and it kind of makes up for a lot. You can talk to him. I wish my father were like that. I wish I had a father like yours."

"He's impossible. But I love him a lot. You love your father, too, I know that."

"But it's not the same. He doesn't act the same with me. We're not close. We never have anything to say to each other that really matters. All we talk about together is sports, how this team is doing or that team. Then he tells me how I should be doing in school and what I want to do with the rest of my life. I don't know what kind of person he is."

"Does anyone? Does your sister?"

"I used to think she did, but then she started to change this year. She's into her rebellion and she's made him very angry. She used to be his pet. They got along much better than he and I did."

"Lots of fathers act strange with their sons."

"How do you know that?"

"From school. When we had visiting weekends, you could see the girls going around hugging their dads, hanging on their arms. The boys didn't kiss their fathers. A lot of them shook hands, and they didn't *talk*. You should have seen Gareth's father. He's about two feet shorter than his son!"

"You actually met him?"

"Once. He came up to school in his limo. He wasn't around for a lot of parent visiting, I guess because he traveled a lot. Like my dad."

"Yeah, but can you tell me exactly what he was like?"

"Why're you so interested?"

Philip shrugged. "Just am, I don't know."

"To tell you the truth, as close as Gareth and I am, I don't know his folks too well. I never got involved with other people's parents because I was too wrapped up in being with mine. In being with my father, I mean. I remember Gareth's father was very funny. Does that help?"

"Funny how? Funny ha-ha or funny strange?"

She shook her head. "Does it really matter?"

"What does he do for a living? Gareth never says, exactly."

Liz laughed. "Do you go around talking about what your father does?"

Actually, he did, or he had at one time. But nobody was terrifically interested in arbitrage, so he'd ended up glossing over his father's occupation. He'd say, "He's in business," and leave it at that. But at least his father was around more than Gareth's or Liz's had been. That was something, he guessed.

By this time, they had reached the UN. The sun had

gone behind the clouds, the day had grown chilly. "Ready to go home now?" he said.

"If you're feeling better. You shouldn't let Claire get to you."

"She always has. The pesky little brother and The Queen."

"She doesn't see herself that way. She writes about herself as if she's afraid."

"What's she afraid of, besides my father getting even more pissed off at her?"

"Oh, she's not afraid of that. That's exactly what she wants, didn't you see that today? At tea? She purposely acted rudely. It's part of her act. She's just testing. Before it's too late."

"For what?"

"Well, when she goes to college she won't be able to try herself out anymore, so she's got to do it now while there's still time, with people who know her."

"How do you know so much?"

Liz shrugged. "Because I'm female, like your sister. Because I lived with females, away from home. And because my father shares his views with me."

Philip never thought of Liz's father with women. He was so independent, so fixed on his own course, it was hard to imagine him sharing his life with anyone. And yet he had Liz, and they were close.

As if she'd read his thoughts, she continued. "I know it sounds odd, because my father never remarried, and he doesn't exactly go out with women, but he's very wise. He was married before, you know, before my mom."

"He was?" She was being very casual about all this. "He told you?"

"We don't have secrets. It was very romantic." She smiled. "They ran away together in college. Well, not exactly ran away. She eloped with him. He was her instructor in a course. They went to Africa afterwards. He was on a grant then, for his doctorate, to do special research. But the marriage didn't last that long. Sometimes I think about it, only because if they'd stayed married to each

59

other I wouldn't have been me. I would have been someone else. Or another me."

"Where is she?" Philip asked.

"I don't know. My father never said. They don't keep in touch or anything."

"No, I guess they wouldn't."

"But still," she sighed, "it was romantic. Eloping and all. When he married my mother they had this big social affair. Church wedding, big tent in the backyard. My mother came from very ritzy people — rich, society types. They thought my father was out of his mind. And I guess they must blame him somehow for my mother dying. They don't talk to us."

"Why would they think that?"

"She died after a trip to Africa. She got some kind of tropical disease from a mosquito bite. They couldn't save her." She stopped walking for a moment and stared down at the sidewalk. "I don't know how we got to talking about my family. This was supposed to be about you." Her eyes were glistening, damp with tears.

"I didn't want to get you upset," Philip said. "I feel awful." Why had she told him this? It was crazy but he was so happy to really know her, to know about her secret things, but at the same time he felt they had gone too far, that it was too intimate for this fragile afternoon. Everything would bend under the weight of this knowledge and break. It frightened him. Nothing like this ever happened in his boring family. "Look, I'm sorry I caused this."

She shook her head. "I wanted to tell you." She squared her shoulders defiantly. "I'm glad." She glanced around. "Hey, is there anyplace we can go and get something to eat? I'm starving."

Philip looked at her. She had that expression on her face again, the one she'd had in her room that day when he'd first kissed her. Expectant. Her mouth opened slightly. Could she mean it? Did she want him to kiss her?

He bent toward her. She closed her eyes. Their lips met, pressed together, and clung. They separated, then he clumsily put his arms around her and held her, for a moment. Inside, happiness, pain, surprise, and joy were mingled indiscriminately. If this was what love was like, then he was in love. Definitely. And he wasn't sorry at all.

CHAPTER NINE

PHILIP DIDN'T TELL HIS PARENTS WHAT HE'D SEEN AND HEARD IN the East Village. He suspected that it wouldn't surprise them, not since Claire had begun her war against the family. But it was too embarrassing to think about explaining what she'd said about them, and the fact that the words had been read aloud in public made it all worse.

First-semester report cards had been handed out and Philip's grades hadn't been too bad. After his initial problems getting used to the workload, he had settled into his accustomed routine of school, friends, and studying, broken up by visits to Liz, an occasional movie, and a few nights hanging out at Gareth's. Gareth claimed never to crack a book, but his grades were better than Philip's or Liz's. "Just a bloody genius," he said, wiggling his eyebrows, but Philip suspected Gareth was a secret crammer; he'd known guys like that at Paley. They pretended not to care, but when exam grades were posted they were the first to see what they got. And crammers also compared their results a lot; they were the ones who said, "Whadja get? Whadja get?" because *their* grades were invariably better.

Philip's parents were less interested in his grades than usual, probably because they figured there was lots of time to worry about where he'd go to college. Right now they were focused on Claire. She didn't want to retake her SATs, she said her scores were perfectly fine from junior year (which they were — she scored well over 1300). "But everyone takes them over," his mom argued, wringing her hands. His father didn't argue. He simply said, "You're taking them and that's final." Though it wasn't the final battle (that was going to be reserved for where she went to college, Philip could see), it certainly felt like it. Philip's grades, respectable and not at all what he'd feared, were lost in the shuffle. His parents nodded, gave him a smile, perused the card, and went back to arguing with Claire.

Given this kind of atmosphere, it was surprising when Philip hit his first obstacle in doing what he pleased. This occurred when he asked his mother if he could attend one of Liz's father's lectures at the museum. "Liz invited me and Gareth. Gareth's going to bring someone too, and we'll have dinner first, there, in one of the big halls, and then there's this talk with a slide show."

His mother didn't answer at first. Her face looked funny, but then she always looked funny these days, with the Claire mess and all. Finally, she said, "I don't know, Phil. It's a school night, you have homework, you're going to be way over on the West Side very late —"

"Gareth and I can split a cab to come home, really, and I can get a lot of my work done after school. I'll come right home." What was her problem? Hadn't she said his grades were good?

"I'll have to speak to your father."

Uh-oh. "Mom, it's *sooooo* important to me, I'll be *sooooo* grateful if you'd let me, honest. You saw my report card, you said my work was fine. It's only one night, really. Please, Mom?" He gave her his best imploring look, the one he used to get ice cream before dinner or another toy from the toy store: "Just one more, Mom, *pleeeeeeze!*"

She knew he was doing what she called "the business" and she smiled. She remembered. They were okay with each other. Then she would say yes, wouldn't she? He couldn't understand why she was hanging back. Didn't she like Liz?

"I know you'd like her dad, if you met him. They're really nice people."

"I'm sure," she said. Was that sarcastic? What was her problem?

"Okay, okay, if you don't want me to I won't go, I'll stay home and be a good boy." He paused. This usually worked, if nothing else did. The old guilt trip.

Bingo. "All right, Philip, but call us if it's going to be really late. I'm going to wait up for you," she warned.

"No sweat," Philip said. Phew, that was tougher than it should have been.

"Is your suit clean?" his mother added. "You're going to have to wear your suit if it's such a big evening function. I want you to look very nice."

"Yeah, okay, Mom," he said. Gareth would probably wear jeans, he figured, because his mom was never around to nag him. He'd just accepted Liz's invitation, right on the spot, really cool. He didn't have to ask, like Philip, and have to say, "Well, I'll check with my parents first." He and Liz had it just right. Life without dumb questions. And arguments over going to stuff you should automatically be allowed to attend. You couldn't say a lecture at a museum was a "waste of time." He didn't understand his parents sometimes. His mother. Women were weird.

His mother had been right. The suit did need cleaning, but he hadn't checked, so he hoped no one was going to notice the stain on the leg of the pants. He thought the bottom of the jacket would hide it, but it didn't. In the good old days, B.C.C. (Before Claire's Craziness), his mother might have checked it out herself and sent the suit in for cleaning. But now ol' Claire had them running around and jumping up and down for her. That was another thing he envied Gareth and Liz — that they didn't have any older sisters or brothers. Being an "only" was cool.

The dinner and lecture were being held in one of the great museum halls, lined with exhibits and dioramas, so that guests could dine while charting the evolution of certain forms of marine life right over their dinner partner's shoulder. Philip and Liz, seated with Gareth and a really gorgeous blonde named Stacey, were up toward the front. At the dais in front, museum officials were seated along with Liz's dad, looking uncomfortable in a dinner jacket and more like a waiter than an eminent scholar, lecturer, and archaeological genius.

"Dad's really nervous tonight," Liz said, leaning over toward him and speaking in a low, intimate voice that thrilled Philip. He made sure his napkin was covering the stain on his pants. Liz looked terrific in a dark dress with a high neck and long sleeves, an odd necklace of metal and beads dipping low over the front of the dress. Liz said it was from some famous tribe, but Philip didn't catch the name. "A gift from a grateful man," she said. "My dad helped the man's wife with some medicine. It was only aspirin but it saved her life, or at least kept her from dying until she could be seen by a doctor."

Philip thought about how Liz's mother had died because no one, not even her dad, could save her, and he wondered if that was why Liz wore the necklace. As if she was reading his mind, Liz said, "It used to belong to my mother."

They were served a mixture of fruit inside a hollowed-out half of a pineapple, soup, salad, and a main course of sliced beef, potatoes, string beans, and grilled tomatoes. After dessert was served (chocolate cake), various museum officials rose and made speeches — some boring, some short, some funny, at least funny to those who understood the references. For Philip and Gareth, it was worse than the gym teacher's efforts to discuss sexually transmitted diseases. Both of them sat back in their chairs and closed their eyes, occasionally, while the girls sat bolt upright, attentive and proper, as the long minutes dragged on. Finally, Liz gave him a poke as her father rose to speak. He was greeted with applause, and he gave a little bow. He spoke the way he did in his own home, his mind roaming from thought to thought, sometimes going off the road for a quick digression, other times returning much later to complete an idea. He was reviewing for his audience some of the major discoveries of his career, and he was going to show everyone some slides to illustrate his great finds.

The lights dimmed and the slides came on. Across the table, Gareth had fallen completely asleep. Stacey was playing with the ends of her long hair, making little braids and undoing them, over and over. Philip wondered if Liz minded. But when he glanced at her he saw that her eyes were glued to the screen.

Slide after slide went by. In some, there were people, shot at a distance, standing near the site of a dig to help indicate the scale. A few times, Philip saw a small child who must have been Liz, though he was never quite sure. The faces of the people were blurred due to the enlargement of the slides being projected. Many of the things pictured were hard to see, because they were almost the same color as the earth in which they lay. Liz's dad picked up a pointer, occasionally, to outline the shape of something special, such as a tool or a piece of a weapon or bowl. The skulls were all in pieces and, in a few cases, hardly looked human at all. Arm, leg, and rib bones were indistinguishable to Philip. Then a slide flashed on, in black and white.

"This was my first major find," Liz's dad said with great pride. "Just put it in for sentimental value."

But Philip wasn't looking at the bones. He was looking at the girl standing near the bones. It must have been Liz's mother. She was so young, and very pretty. Her arm was raised over her forehead to shield her eyes from the sun, even though she had on a hat. But you could see she was nice-looking. Philip stared at her, trying to learn a little about Liz. She didn't look like her daughter, though. She kind of looked a little like old pictures of Philip's mom, but that was probably because everyone wore the same hairstyles then or something. The slide disappeared from the screen, replaced by another.

66

He glanced at Liz to see if she was upset at seeing her mother on the screen. But Liz was frowning, slightly, looking down at her hands. She didn't seem upset, more annoyed than anything else. Maybe that was how she handled all of those feelings. He leaned over toward her.

"Your mom was very pretty," he whispered.

She looked right up at him. "What?" she whispered sharply.

"Your mom," he repeated. "Up there, on the screen, was pretty."

"Where?"

"In that slide," he said. Some of the people at a nearby table were giving him dirty looks, so he pointed. On the screen, at that moment, was some statue of a pregnant lady, some fertility goddess, her dad was saying. She thought he was making a joke, so she laughed. He was going to have to wait until the lecture was over.

But when the talk ended, and everyone applauded long and loud for several minutes, Liz disappeared and went to her father's side. Philip followed shyly and was greeted with a warm handshake. "So, how did you enjoy my little fireside chat?"

Before Philip could answer, someone pulled Liz's dad away and Philip was surrounded by more members of the audience wishing to shake this famous man's hand. He looked for Liz and when he caught her eye, signaled that he would be waiting for her near the door. Glancing around he caught sight of Gareth's tall figure moving toward the exit, one long arm wrapped around Stacey. He called out to Gareth but his friend couldn't hear in the post-lecture babble of voices. There goes the shared cab, he thought, glancing at his watch. It was very late, much later than he'd told his parents. He went to look for a phone.

67

CHAPTER TEN

His parents were pissed, so it was a piece of luck that when he hung up the pay phone he caught sight of Liz. She probably knew where Gareth was, and they'd catch their cab and he could get home and explain what a long evening it was, blah-blah, but he'd learned so much about anthropology, blah-blah, bones and bowls and roast beef for dinner too.

"I don't know," she told Philip when he asked about their friend's whereabouts.

"Guess I'm on my own." He realized she was waiting for him to say something, about the evening and about how terrific her father was, which he was, really. But when he opened his mouth to tell her, he found something else coming out instead. "Liz, that picture on the slide . . . You know, the one with the lady doing this?" He threw his arm up as if to shade his eyes from the hot sun. What was it about that picture? What was it he wanted to know? "Was that your mom?"

She wrinkled her eyes a little. It must be tough to think about a dead parent, Philip realized, and he felt dumb. It was stupid to be curious about her mother. He'd never meet her, so what was the point? But there was something he had to know, absolutely. Liz looked at him, hard, then said, "I think you must mean his first wife."

Oh, the famous first wife, the one she'd told him

about when they were coming home from the East Village. Except then she'd been real open about it. Now her face looked tight and secretive. So that pretty lady on the screen had been the first wife. And Liz probably did mind it, because it meant her mom had been second and all.

"Ohhh," Philip said. "I was just wondering, because —"

"It's not such a big deal," Liz said, but her face said it was a big deal. Why had she been so different about it that day?

Her father came up and threw one arm around Liz and the other around Philip. He was sweaty and disheveled. "Well, that's finished. Did it bore you to tears? To sleep, perchance to dream? Howdja like my traveling road show? And did you check out baby Lizzie in those old shots?"

"He was just asking about, you know, the slide, Dad."

"You know the slide what?" her father said. He was looking at Liz as if she were crazy or something.

"Your slide . . ." Philip said, wanting to be ultra cool and grown-up about this. After all, how many people did he know that he could look straight in the eye and deliver the next line to? "Your first wife."

He was positive, just then, that Liz stuck her elbow into her father's side, just a nudge. What was going on here?

"Oh, yes, well that was just a lovely romance, right out of college. Lovely romance, lovely person. It didn't really last long, and of course nowadays you young people don't seem to need to get married to authorize things." He paused and cleared his throat. "But Liz, I swear, if you ever —" And she laughed and the subject, it seemed, was closed.

Philip's mother opened the door to the apartment. She was really angry. He hesitated before stepping inside, wondering how he could avoid what promised to be a bad scene.

"Just how do you think you're going to be able to get up and make it to school on time?" she said. Her foot, shod in her soft slipper, tapped on the marble foyer floor. It sounded like a little dance, rap-a-tap-tap, muffled but nerve-wracking all the same. He was accustomed to getting along with his mother; the world turned upside-down when he was not.

"Aw, gee, Ma," was all he could say. This was no time to start in on the educational evening pitch. Education was irrelevant. It was late.

"I'm going to ground you this weekend," she went on, rap-a-tap-tapping that foot.

"Just for being a little late?" He was going to have to bargain fast. A whole weekend meant no Liz, no Gareth, no movies, no adventures hanging out at Liz's apartment. Two days of horrible Claire, his workaholic dad, and his angry mom. "C'mon, Ma, you know I'll never do that again."

"It's final," she said. She was really, really angry this time. What got her so pissed off? That he had a good time with someone else? That he liked Liz's father and wanted to hear him speak? That he was sort of in love with Liz? Maybe Freud was right and mothers were jealous of sons. Old Oedipus Rex and all that jazz.

"Get!" she said, pointing a long finger in the direction of his room.

He got.

And he wondered, for the rest of the week, what all of this sound and fury was supposed to mean. His mother had never been so strict with him before. His father, yes, but not his mother. Especially not lately, with Claire and all her problems being given the prime-time slot. He forgot about the talk and the slide show, and when he saw Liz he didn't even ask about the curious first wife who had aroused such interest in him.

Stuck at home on Saturday, however, listening to the sound of his clock in the silence as steady as a faucet dripping, he was aware of how alone he was and the image of the lady in the slide rose before him, unbidden. Her arm over her face, dressed in her desert clothes, something familiar in her ghostly presence. She was the skeleton in Liz's family closet.

Liz was very sympathetic about being somewhat the cause of his being grounded. "Poor baby," she had said, as she patted his cheek. He wasn't even allowed to call her, supposedly, though if he did right now who would know? His mother had gone out shopping, his dad had gone to do something at the office even though it was a Saturday (the man never stopped), and Claire? Who knew what Claire was up to these days? She disappeared like a wraith, slipping through doors virtually unnoticed. Her old friends didn't even come around anymore. Claire had only new friends, "new people," she called them.

He lay on his bed contemplating how nothing seemed easy anymore. And then the image of the woman in the slide returned. He got up from his bed and walked out of his room, down the hall, and into the living room. Along one wall was a set of bookcases. Below waist level was a ledge on which his mother displayed vases, photographs in frames, small crystal birds, and one or two lopsided clay creations he and Claire had brought home at various stages in elementary school art. Beneath the ledge were several sets of double doors, concealing what his mother called "family junk": scrapbooks, boxes of photos, old yearbooks, manila envelopes stuffed with report cards, finger paintings, homemade birthday cards, his and Claire's efforts all jumbled together. Without really knowing what he was looking for he started to search among the piles, finally pulling out the bottom half of a cardboard box in which a heap of photos lay, mixed in with loose negatives, photo envelopes, and old Christmas cards.

Many of the pictures were of people Philip scarcely knew or couldn't recognize at all. Family friends from their old neighborhood, faded photos of aging relatives who were nameless and faceless. His mother would hold up these pictures and squint at them, when challenged to identify the subject. "I think this is your great-uncle Edward on your father's mother's side." She'd tap the edge of the photo against her forehead as if it could telepathically communicate its secrets to her. Usually, she was right. She had a great memory. Now, shuffling through this box of pictures was like trying to read a book in a foreign language; it was indecipherable. Yet everyone here was connected somehow to his life. His mother had always threatened to put these things into an album one day and label them, so her kids would know who everyone was. But she never had the time. At least she said she never had the time. Now he wished she had.

Why? Because he was looking for something, a missed connection that he had to find. He removed a second box from beneath a pile of old *National Geographic* magazines and searched further. He found some old snapshots of his mother dressed in a summer camp uniform, posing in front of cabins, at a lakefront with friends. She looked about twelve or thirteen, but it was hard to tell. Young girls looked older with their funny hair and clothes. But he guessed that girls his own age must look equally strange, because so many wore a lot of make-up, heavy jewelry hanging down, things his mother would not have been permitted to use or wear.

Eventually, he grew tired of this search and of all the strange faces squinting up at so many different cameras. Only a few photos were even fairly recent; several were his sister and himself as babies; his parents looked astonishingly different and astonishingly the same. He shoved the boxes of photos back inside the cabinet any which way. No one would notice the disarray; they hardly ever opened these doors.

In the next cabinet, he found his father's high school yearbook. His father looked shockingly young and a little like Philip. Philip swallowed hard as he stared at the photo. He felt he didn't know this young man any better than he knew the person who was now his father. Did it say "workaholic" next to his photo? Nope. It said, "Class

Clown." Class Clown? His father? Must be some mistake. No, that's what it said, along with Honor Society, Key Club, Chemistry Club, Basketball. Basketball? He never talked about playing basketball. Is that why his dad always wanted to go see the Knicks?

The next yearbook in the pile must have belonged to a relative. His mother and father were missing from it. He went down the pile, his father in college, his father in law school, some recent yearbooks from Claire's private school, his own from Paley this past spring. His mother's were missing. He looked again. There was one yearbook that she wasn't in.

Suddenly, he thought it, all at once. He turned the pages of the yearbook, senior year, Cornell University. And, of course, just like in the movies when they find the missing clue, there it was. There *she* was. The face of the lady in the slide. And the name of the lady in the slide: OLIVIA ROBBINS COOKE.

The answer was just what he'd been afraid of, just what he probably knew when he saw the picture and then Liz gave her dad the elbow — shhh, he doesn't know. They thought he was a jerk because he didn't know. His own mother knew, she never told him. What if they had stayed married . . . that man could have been his *father*? And Liz would have been, oh God, his *sister*? This was too much. This was definitely too much. His mother had never lied to him before. Never, not once. He had known that. He had trusted her. No wonder she was not happy with Liz. No wonder she didn't want him at any slide show, or even hanging around that apartment. What a piece of bad luck for her. For *her*? What about *him*?

His heart was going a million miles a minute. It was as if he couldn't take a breath even if he wanted to. He felt lied to and cheated. Maybe his father didn't even know. Of course he'd have to know, there was the damn yearbook right in the house, and who knows what else? Letters? Love letters? Their marriage license? Wedding pictures? He'd seen his parents' wedding pictures. How come she'd worn white then, a real bride's dress? To fool her children into thinking it was the first time? Philip felt an enormous sense of disgust.

Leaving the books in a pile on the living room floor, he walked back down the hall and into his parents' bedroom. It was calm and cool and, just the same as when he was a small child, an enormous sense of peace and security came over him when he entered their room. The bed was made, the spread pulled up, and on each side of the bed, on the night tables, was a pile of books and magazines that his parents were reading. He opened a closet door, his father's. The suits hung in a straight line, the shoes in neat, gleaming rows. He always had them polished downtown, by the same man on the street, for years. Philip had met the man a few times when he had gone with his father on a school holiday, to the office for a short visit, and then out to lunch. They always ate at the same place, a French restaurant, something de la Croix, and Philip always ate mashed potatoes and chicken with wine. Then they'd come out and go to the shoeshine man, Jimmy, and Philip's shoes would be shined too. This was the ritual until Philip began to wear sneakers everywhere and got too old to go to Daddy's office. He felt a kind of regret for their lost time together, and now that everything was changing Philip knew it was a time that would never come again. It was now The Time Before He Knew.

His mother's closet smelled of her perfume. Piles of sweaters were arranged neatly on shelves and her clothes, of different shapes and sizes, hung in a more colorful disarray than his dad's. He closed the door and moved to her night table. He opened the top drawer. He used to come in and rummage around in here when he was younger and needed something — a pen, scissors, or a pad — that he didn't have in his room. Now older, he had all of his own supplies and didn't go into people's drawers for things. His mom was very big on privacy. That thought made him smirk. Sure, privacy. Don't tell.

The top drawer had the same assortment of things as it had always contained: scissors, needle and thread, pencils, pens, pads, playing cards, coupons she'd clipped, letters, scribbled notes to herself. He fished through the jumble, but nothing seemed old. It was all recent. The next drawer contained a supply of stationery, personalized with his mother's name and address. Its familiar pale blue color raised a load of memories in Philip, of all the letters she'd written to him in summer camp for so many years — long, loyal letters that had made him feel so good. He'd even saved them somewhere, in a pile, stuck in an old zippered canvas bag in the back of his closet.

In the bottom drawer, he found what he wanted. Piles of personal papers, stacked to the top of the drawer, some held together with rubber bands, string, ribbons, in no particular order. He looked through the first bunch of papers near the top; they were overseas airmail envelopes, the edges frayed, the handwriting very small as if the person who wrote them had attempted to use every fraction of an inch of letter space to cram in thoughts. Philip squinted at the writing, and then turned over the envelope, to see to whom it was addressed and to check the stamp and the postmark.

"What are you doing?" His mother. He hadn't heard her.

He was trapped. He'd been found out. All at once his shame and his embarrassment mixed with his outrage at how he'd been humiliated and lied to. He dropped the papers and stood up to face her. He opened his mouth to tell her how angry he was but instead of words a kind of strangled cry came out. He burst into tears and fled from her room.

CHAPTER ELEVEN

"OPEN UP YOUR DOOR . . . NOW!" CAME HIS MOTHER'S VOICE. He'd never heard her so angry.

He did not answer. She knocked several times, waited, then repeated her order to him to open his door.

Why should he open it? What did they have to talk about? Sure, it was a rotten thing to do, to go through someone's private stuff, but look what she'd done to him. She'd lied to him about something so big it made him look ridiculous for not knowing. She'd made herself out to be someone she wasn't. His own mother. Not married to his dad first, as they'd always pretended. They'd even talked about when they met, and went on their first date, and everything. Nobody had ever said it hadn't been someone's first marriage.

He couldn't even begin to think about Liz. And worst of all, Liz's dad. He was so mixed-up about that part. Now, instead of being the guy that maybe he would have liked to have for a father, he had become the guy who just very well might have been his father. It made him feel sick to think about kissing Liz, since she was nearly a relative. And he'd thought her dad was a friend. How could he be friends with someone who'd been married — married! — to his own mom? Surely he must have known who Philip's mom was. Liz had even met her. Liz knew, she had to. She was the worst liar of them all.

His mother had gone away from his door. He'd never forgive her for this, never. She had ruined everything, totally. They simply wouldn't ever speak. There wasn't anything to say, so why bother? This was the worst, worst thing that had ever happened to him, that could ever happen to him.

Lucky Claire. She got to go away to college next year, not have to live in the house anymore. Claire. Did she know too? Was he the only idiot in the family who was kept in the dark? He moved close to the wall near his bed to listen for sounds from her room. It was quiet. He'd ask her later.

He leaned back, with his head against the pillows, and stared at the spot on the ceiling that he sometimes focused on when he was doing serious thinking. The spot was small and Philip had to squint sometimes to see it, depending on the time of day and how much light there was in the room. The spot resembled, alternately, a dragon, a stalk of celery, or a submarine, the last only if you twisted your head and looked at it upside down. As Philip stared at the spot, now looking for all the world like a fire-breathing, roaring dragon, he felt his eyes fill with tears. Something was ruined for him, terribly damaged, and he believed it would never be repaired again. It, whatever it was, had come to an end. And now he was going to have to get on with his life, but everything was different.

Maybe he should leave for a while, go over and stay with Gareth, until he knew how he could face things. He could pack a small bag, go inside, call his friend, and then casually announce to his dad that he was going to have a sleepover at a friend's. His dad didn't usually give him permission for such things but maybe he would today. Then Philip could leave the house without speaking to his mother at all.

His mother. He kept seeing the face in the yearbook picture superimposed over the one in the slide. Olivia Cooke, fancy that. Of all the jerks in the whole world to marry, she had to pick the father of his first girlfriend. What a piece of rotten luck.

The spot now looked like celery, and the idea of going to Gareth's was very attractive. He got up and unlocked his bedroom door, opening it just enough to listen for sounds of footsteps. He still wanted to ask Claire if she'd known. But he could see that the door to her room was open and her light wasn't on. Tiptoeing into the hall, he strained to listen for sounds of his parents, deciding to make a mad dash into the kitchen via the dining room to use the phone near the refrigerator.

Just as he was about to take off, he heard the sound of someone crying. His mother, it had to be. And just like when he was little and he'd done something absolutely frightful that had made her cry, he was washed by a wave of guilt so powerful it made his knees shake. The sobbing was pitiful and so very sad. He moved quietly to the corner of the hall near her bedroom door, which was ajar. Then he peered in.

She was sitting on the bed, next to the open drawer filled with the letters and papers. She was holding some of the letters in her hand, and she was crying her heart out, not loudly but steadily, holding tightly to those letters. An electric shock went through him. She still loved him! That's what all of this was about. She was still in love with her first husband, with Liz's dad. And that made a whole lot of sense because even he liked Liz's dad more than his own father. Right now, his poor father was slaving away at the office on a Saturday while his wife sat crying over old love letters from Africa!

"Philip," she said. She'd seen him. It was all over. She wiped her face with a swift motion, drawing both hands down over her eyes and then her cheeks. "It's a terrible thing to come home and find your child going through your things." She gestured toward the drawer.

He shrugged. What did it matter in light of all the truly enormous things he'd found out?

"But," she went on, "it's not nearly as awful as coming home and finding two letters from your other child, one for her mother and one for her father, explaining why she has run away!"

78

She held up the letters. They weren't love letters at all. They were from Claire, and she'd run away — today, now. And that stupid, obnoxious, punked-out sister of his had completely stolen his thunder. His mother didn't know what he'd discovered, didn't care. She was crying about Claire. Of all the disgusting tricks, of all the rotten betrayals that the day had held, this was the worst.

"I'm going, Ma," he said.

"Phil . . . Philip, do you know where she might be? Do you know who this friend is she talks about, Simon Something-or-Other, I can't read her writing — " She broke off and came after him as he stepped into his room to grab his jacket. "Are you running away too? At least tell me where you're going," she demanded.

"Out, Mom, to a friend's."

"But where? You have to tell me. I can't take any more secrecy from you kids. This is a perfectly frightening city and to have the two of you at large is just too much for me to handle right now." She started to cry again. Philip felt bad for her, but worse for himself. This was no time to start telling her what was bothering him. He just had to get away, to go somewhere he could talk, see someone. But who? Surely *not* Liz. Or her dad.

"I don't know. Maybe Gareth, maybe one of my old friends from Paley." He softened. "Don't worry, I'll be home later. I'm not going to pull a Claire." *At least not yet*, he thought. He believed he could understand why she had gotten so freaky these last months.

"But just tell me," she said, "if you know where she might be, it would really help me. I don't know where to begin looking. She's mad at her father over all this business about college applications. He's been pushing her too hard, I know that, but she's been wrong too. She shouldn't throw away three years of work on a whim. I want to be able to tell her that what she's doing isn't necessary. We will . . . he will . . . listen to her and try to adjust his ideas accordingly. She can go to California if she wants." His mother ran out of breath and ended her speech with a defeated sigh, shoulders drooping.

He almost reached over to give her a pat, make her feel it would be okay. Then he remembered how furious he was and he withdrew his hand.

"I'll be back later."

"Do you know anyone we could call?" she said.

"If I think of anything, I'll let you know." He sounded as impersonal as a telephone operator. He wanted her to notice that he was in trouble, that he was in pain. Claire wasn't the only child in this household, even though she did seem to get all of the attention. Weren't there any trophies for the good kid?

He left her there, standing in the hall, staring at those letters and trying to find a tiny clue to her daughter's whereabouts. Going out the door, Philip wondered also where the hell his sister could be, because if he could disappear right now and never come back, he'd do it too.

———————

Wandering around New York City in the winter was a real drag. How could you think with piles of rain-soaked garbage backing up puddles into tiny rivers that sopped through your sneakers into your socks, while a steady drizzle fell onto your neck and hair and chilled you to the bone?

Still, Philip's surroundings were appropriate; they matched his mood, much as a dark and stormy night was the correct setting for a Dracula movie. Drowned rat seemed just the right image. It suited his feeling of slinking around, rain-soaked and surreptitious, looking for a place to hide.

But why did he feel so dirty? This wasn't his fault. It was some kind of conspiracy, a conspiracy of grown-ups (except for Liz but he couldn't think of her right now, that hurt too damn much). The shock of discovery about his mother was hard enough to deal with. He didn't want to get into all the other stuff that involved Liz's role.

Jumping on the crosstown bus, Philip rode it to the river and walked over to the promenade. Few people were out on this chilly, rainy Saturday. Briefly and angrily he wondered where his sister was. He knew that was all his parents really cared about right now. They had no idea that *he* was in pain, that he had a problem they needed to be concerned about. *Boy, I am really the second child in this family,* he thought as he skirted the puddles and stared at the gray river water. Until the thing with Claire was straightened out, which was probably going to be never, they wouldn't bother to listen to him. Funny thing about Claire was, she managed to get their total attention when she was doing her good and terrific number. And now that she was being horrid, she was at the center just the same.

They really don't care how I am or what I do, not really.

Thinking of Liz's father just then, he realized that he had lost a chance to be friends with him. Kenneth Cooke had been part of the betrayal, too, maybe the center. And he had proved himself to be just another rotten person in the process. The hurt there was almost the strongest. He had wanted something from Ken: a second chance with another father? Ken might have *been* his father, for Chrissakes. It made his skin crawl, thinking about it. His mom and her dad. They had been together. They had been young and in love. They had married when they were in college and she had been at the site of his first major discovery. Then they had divorced. Did they hate each other? Were they secret friends? Had either one of them ever gotten over it? He tried to imagine if he had grown up and married Liz, and then divorced, and his kid had become a teenager and met her kid — never mind. The complications tangled in each other, like so many pieces of colored thread in a sewing basket, making a ball of endless pieces that you had to throw away because none of it was useful anymore.

He had wanted Ken to be his real father.

That was the center of the hurt, the painful, glowing core in his chest that would pulse with a painful thrust and cause him to catch his breath. He had wanted this as much as he had wanted to be close to Liz. He wanted both of them; it was like a double falling in love. More than friendship, he knew, he wanted a connection to this man.

Well, now he'd gotten it — the connection. And it made him sick to his stomach. He sat down on one of the wet benches that faced the river and put his head in his hands. He wanted to cry again, out here, with no one watching. But all he could feel was that heavy lump in his chest, pulsing with pain and emitting its strange glow that made him feel flushed and hot even though he was wet and cold.

CHAPTER TWELVE

"IT's NO PROBLEM," GARETH SAID. "NO SWEAT. NO ONE'S EVEN home." He held his apartment door open and Philip entered into that modern fairyland. Some kind of weird light sculpture had been installed in the entrance hall and it glowed green and eerie, making a funny neon noise as they went past, a burning zzzzziiizzz. Philip made a wide circle around it; he thought it was going to explode.

"You're soaked. Want to change your clothes?" Gareth said. He was wearing one of his crazy t-shirts, this one saying, AUNTIE EM, HATE KANSAS, TAKING DOG, DOROTHY. How would this giant's clothing fit him? Philip shook his head.

"At least I'll give you a towel. And take off your sneakers, buddy. You're making a puddle on the rug."

Philip yanked off his offending Nikes and put them near the front door. Gareth's place was always so cold and so perfect, as if no one lived there, ever. No signs of habitation, at least not in the public rooms. Gareth's room was an unholy mess. But Philip could understand. If this was his parents' place, he'd want to hole up in his room all the time too.

Gareth returned with a big, black oversized bath towel. Philip never knew anyone with black towels, and they seemed the essence of weirdness. All of the strange fantasies he'd had about Gareth's parents came to the fore. Drug smugglers, CIA agents, Russian spies, art forgers. Why had he never met them? Why were they never home? And who took care of Gareth? Suddenly, all these questions seemed exquisitely pertinent. He had to know about his friend's family. Maybe their strangeness would mirror the sudden craziness that had emerged in his own household.

"So, um, Gareth, how's it going? How come you're not out today? I mean, I'm glad you were home. Lucky I caught you to visit and everything."

"Phil, you're blabbering. What's up? You look terrible."

He couldn't say. At once, he was aware of Gareth's long-term connection to Liz. Supposing Gareth was in on it too? And what was he going to say? My mom and her dad? What? Would Gareth care about it the way he did? Looking at it from his friend's point of view the whole thing seemed trivial and silly, like a bit of boring, stale gossip. He said the first thing he could think of, unconnected to his pain. "Claire, my sister, ran away."

"Really?" Gareth answered. "The punky one?"

"Yeah. But they don't know where. They got letters."

"Freakin' them out, right? Can you help?"

"Who me? Naw, she never tells me anything. Except for that one time when I went to hear her read, remember?"

"Yeah, the stuff about you and your family. You never said if it was any good."

"Oh, it was good all right. If only it wasn't us she was talking about. Claire was full of surprises that day. In fact, she's been going through something big this year, right in front of our eyes . . . a transformation."

"Do you like her better this way?"

He thought a moment. "No . . . Yes . . . I don't know. Maybe. It's hard living with someone who's just become weird."

"As opposed to someone weird right off the bat, right?" Gareth laughed. "You should meet my folks."

"Where are they?"

"Gallery opening in Soho. They're always at gallery openings. Or on a plane. Or at auctions. Or out at parties. They're famous, in their circle of friends. The great art collectors and patrons of whatever turns them on."

"I'd like to meet them," Philip said.

"No you wouldn't. They're real boring."

Philip almost said, "My parents are too," but he stopped then and remembered. No, you couldn't call them boring right now. They were frighteningly interesting, all of a sudden, but not in the way you wanted your parents to be interesting.

"Well, I'd still like to meet them one day."

"They're short," Gareth said.

"Everybody looks short to you."

"No, honest. They are both extremely short individuals. You'd be very surprised."

"What does your father do, actually, besides the art thing?"

"And being short."

"Yeah, being short."

"He dabbles."

"In what?"

"This and that."

"You're always so evasive when I ask you about him. And he's never here, so —"

Gareth shrugged. "Listen, if I knew, I'd tell you. It's always something different. He just buys stuff no one wants and then he turns around and sells it to someone who wants it. Import-export."

"You mean, like leftover Statue of Liberty erasers, or Cabbage Patch dolls?"

"No, not things. Stuff. In bulk. Commodities."

"I don't know what the hell you're talking about. I give up." Philip realized, then, the way his friends must have felt when he was trying to explain arbitrage. They knew that he didn't know what he was talking about, so they asked a lot of questions which he really couldn't answer, and they got into this endless circle of talk that went nowhere.

"Seeing Liz?" Gareth asked.

"No."

"Hey, don't jump down my throat. Something wrong there? That why you're looking like you want a fight?"

"No. I'm not seeing her."

"At all?"

Philip didn't answer.

"Okay, I'm dropping the subject. But she does really like you. You know that. She doesn't get that close to many people, even though she has an amazing amount of friends. She's, like, always *protecting* herself."

"Yeah," Philip said curtly.

"That bad, huh? I'm staying out of this one. Want to go out for a hamburger? Are you dry yet?"

"I'm going, Gareth, I gotta get home to my parents. They're probably thinking I ran away too, or something. Listen, thanks for having me over."

"Will you cut the crap? You don't have to do that kind of thing with me. We're friends. If you want to come in dripping wet and ask me questions about my folks, which is really boring to me but okay I'll answer them, and not tell me why you're mad as hell at Liz and not talk about what's eating at you, that's all right. I'm not going to sit in judgment. One day, though, you have to return the favor. I'll ask you boring questions and not tell you what's the matter, all right?"

"Gareth, your parents bore you, but do you trust them? Do they tell you the truth?"

"You *are* crazy. Whoever said parents were supposed to tell their kids the truth? Do you tell your parents the truth?"

"But if they lie to you —"

"Parents always lie. It's part of the job description."

"But if it's something big . . . ."

"I guess if they tell you you're a girl and you're really a boy, it might screw you up. Is that what this is all about? They lied to you? You mean you aren't going to inherit two million dollars? Don't get so worked up. Maybe you were better off with the lie."

86

Gareth was right. He was. But whose fault was it that he'd found out?

He decided then, in an instant, that he would go see Liz.

It wasn't Liz who opened the apartment door. It was him. Kenneth Cooke. Her dad.

Philip's face flushed and his heart thundered in his chest. Now what? Part of him wanted to turn away and run to the elevator. But then he'd have to push the button and wait for it to come. No, he couldn't make a clean getaway in a New York City apartment building. No way. So he just stood on the straw doormat outside the front door of the apartment and shuffled from foot to foot.

It was possible her father didn't notice. He wasn't exactly totally aware of things that were going on in the world, especially when he was wrapped up in some new weird discovery. Philip hoped he'd find him that way, preoccupied and out of sorts, and then he could come in and have it out with Liz. But no luck. Funny how the full force of this man's attention used to seem incredibly flattering to Philip but now it was distasteful. Philip wanted to hit him.

"I'm afraid you're out of luck. Liz got a phone call a while ago and went scooting out of here. I think it was a girlfriend of hers, someone in trouble it seemed. Come in," he said finally, remembering his manners.

"I, uh, it was just Liz . . . I really gotta be going," Philip stammered like a jerk. Say it. Say, *you betrayed me. Both of you. All three of you, including her, my mother. My own mother.*

Kenneth stared at him. For a second, Philip thought it would happen. The man would start to explain, then Philip would sock him in the jaw. He'd never hit anyone really hard in his life, maybe in the playground when he was little, once, when this big boy tried to steal his bicycle. He could recall the funny mushy feeling of the kid's skin under his fist, not hard like in the movies when there was a "bam" with each punch, but something curiously silent instead, silent and soft. His fist was probably too weak to make an impression on this man's face. And he was much stronger than a kid in the park.

"Hey, fella, what's this? What's going on?" Angry and confused, Philip had raised his arm and pulled it back. Kenneth caught his wrist and held it firmly. "Has something happened? Are you all right?"

The hurt and anger welled up in Philip until he couldn't stand it any longer. "I hate you," he blurted out. "I hate you and I hate her, I hate her so much."

"Come inside, Phil. Come on, come with me." Kenneth's voice was very firm but gentle, the way he must talk to those weird tribesmen and gain their trust, Philip thought, as he allowed himself to be led inside the apartment and into the kitchen, where Kenneth sat him down on a stool and asked him if he'd like something to drink. Funny, he didn't get into all the obvious questions, like why Philip hated him and why Philip hated Liz, though maybe he didn't mean Liz — maybe he meant his mother. Her. Could be either one. But he was sure all the same that this man knew what he was talking about. He'd known it all along, and that thought made Philip burn with shame.

Philip sipped a Coke. Kenneth kept looking at him with his peculiar expression of firmness and concern, and after a while Philip wanted to tell him, in spite of the fact that he must already know.

"My mom . . ." he began, and he studied Kenneth's face for some sign of recognition of this enormous problem. But his expression didn't change. Still steady, still concerned.

"My mom and you . . ." he said.

Kenneth's face loomed in front of his, suffused with caring.

"Were married," Philip said with a half-sob.

"Uh-huh," Kenneth said. "And . . ." he prompted.

"That's it!"

"That's it? That's what this I-hate-you-and-you-want-to-slug-me-and-you-hate-her is all about? Why? Have you talked to her about this? Is there something I should know?"

"You never told me."

"I never told you?"

"Well, I mean, she never did. And Liz knew and then I saw the slide —"

"Hold it. Let's go back a little. Take a drink of Coke and I'll run this by you. Your mother never told you that she and I had been married, right?"

Philip nodded.

"Okay. And you assumed that when Liz met you she knew from me all about this mystery from the past and that she conspired with me to keep it from you. Having ascertained first, of course, that you didn't know. Right?"

Philip nodded again. He thought that was how he felt, but he wasn't sure. Did he believe Liz had always known?

"But did she know?" Philip asked.

"No. Not then. We don't exactly go over this every night. No offense, Philip, but the past is the past. Your mother and I had our differences and we resolved them in our own way. Then we both walked away. The fact that our children stumbled onto a friendship with each other . . ." He shrugged. "Call it fate. Karma. Kismet. An accident. A pleasure. I like you. And that's separate from who you happen to be related to. But I can see from the expression on your face that you think this was a dirty, sordid, ugly trick on all our parts."

Philip turned away. The truth was that he did feel dirty. "It's her fault," he said softly.

"Liz? No . . . your mother?"

Philip nodded.

"Why?"

"Because she misled us. She made us think there was only my dad."

"So you're angry because of your dad. Your dad had the right to be married to her first."

"No, I don't feel that way. I'm angry because she lied to us. To me."

"Surely not to him."

"We thought there hadn't been another . . . another husband."

"But what if we'd lived together? Would that have troubled you?"

"Married is different."

"You're right there, young man, right on the money. Which is precisely the reason we got divorced."

"Money?"

"No. Because marriage is different. Marriage is 'you're stuck with what you've got.' And we two were very unsuited but didn't find out until after. Your mother was the most enchanting female I have ever known, including Liz's mother, but you don't have to tell Liz. And she was crazy about me — big white hunter image and all that, explorer in the wild. But take a lady who needs museums and bookstores and music and stick her out in the middle of the desert somewhere and what you have, eventually, is a parting of the ways."

"That can't be all . . . just different views." Philip experienced a combination of very sophisticated feelings, being talked to in such a way, and an edge of suspicion that he was being lied to or, at best, misled again. Brought to see things in a certain way. People thought they could fool teenagers all the time, screw around with their heads.

"Your mother's a trouper, she is. I'm glad she's happy now," Kenneth said, riding over Philip's disbelief. His response stopped Philip cold. Happy? His mother happy? He never thought of her that way, in that particular state. She was . . . she was . . . what was she? She was his mother. She was married. She was what she was. Was she happy? He wondered if anyone married to his father could exist in a state you could call happy. Why, he himself was rarely happy, except maybe when he and Liz —

"But Liz knew," he blurted out. "She knew and she never told me."

"Liz probably likes you more than she's said," Kenneth pointed out. "When you feel that way, I'm sure you don't go around upsetting apple carts. You pick and choose what you tell someone very carefully. Whatever she did do, she did because she thought you had to be protected."

Philip wasn't sure if he'd heard the front door slam, but he knew when the footsteps approached that it was Liz, coming into the kitchen. He prepared to turn around on his seat and confront her, but just as he was about to move he heard the other voice, then the laughing, and he realized she was with someone.

When he did turn around he saw Liz coming into the kitchen, followed by his sister Claire — runaway Claire, who'd stolen all the attention in his family — smirking and strutting in her grotesque punk finery. She was smiling at him. And Liz was smiling too. What the hell were they doing together? Had everyone in the world turned against him?

Without a word he got up and left the kitchen, left the apartment, because there was nothing he could say anymore, ever, to these people.

CHAPTER THIRTEEN

SHIVERING AND SOAKED, PHILIP FINALLY RETURNED HOME. There was no point in staying out all night. There was no point in trying to make any more sense out of what happened. Quite simply, his mother had ruined his relationship with Liz and her father, Claire had made it a shambles, and his father had screwed up everything that had come before. Where he had thought, previously, that he had an okay home life and a girl who really might be in love with him, now he had nothing.

The sound of his key in the lock must have brought his parents into the hall at once, because there they were, standing in the doorway to the living room, looking older and more tired than usual. They didn't ask where he had been, didn't comment on the fact that the hour was far later than his accustomed time of return. His mother tried to come over and hug him, but he pushed her away, gently. He knew he was acting pricky but he didn't care. Let *them* worry about me for once, he thought.

"I saw Claire," he said over his shoulder as he headed for the kitchen to get something to eat.

"She's here," his father said. "She's in her room." Then he hesitated. Philip felt real sorry for his father. He felt that his dad had been betrayed, too, though he wasn't sure why. "Philip, we're glad to see you. Claire told us you were upset."

Philip whirled around. "Claire? Claire told you? Is that what it's come down to here, that my feelings and my situation come down to you from my sister, who gets most of the attention anyway? What do you mean Claire told you? How do you know she isn't lying to you anyway, just like she does all the time these days? Or do you still think she's Miss Perfect, the Golden Girl?"

His father had drawn back from him, as if Philip had slugged him. He hadn't meant to yell at his dad, of all people. Why had he gone and done that?

"She only said you'd had a fight with your girlfriend," his father said in a quiet voice. Philip didn't look at his mother. She hadn't said a word.

"Oh," his voice was sarcastic. "So that's all she told you."

"Philip," his mother's voice. Talking at last. What was she going to say? He turned his head away. "Why were you going through my drawers?"

The anger came over him again. "Why? Why did Claire run away? Why did she write a book about us, talking about how stupid and creepy we all are? Hasn't she shown it to you? Don't you want to see it? Why didn't you tell me you'd been married before? To *him*?"

Furious, he turned and stormed off to his room, slamming the door, then locking it. There was nothing anyone could say that was going to make a difference. And if he saw Claire, he was going to kill her. She, too, was part of the plot. She was in on this, taking over his relationship with Liz, running away from home and *to their house*, of all places. He threw himself onto his bed and curled into a ball. How was he going to live with these people after this?

Exhausted and cold, he fell asleep in his damp clothing and believed he heard nothing throughout the rest of the night — no one tapping on his door, no one trying to resolve the problem. He slept until after noon on Sunday, waking up to his filthy room, crumpled and smelly clothes, and the start of what he knew was going to be a perfectly awful cold.

There were a few pieces of paper shoved beneath his door. One said, "Liz called twice, call her back." This was in his mother's handwriting. Another had his name printed on the front, from Claire. He wanted to tear it up but he read it first. "Don't jump to conclusions," it said. "Let's have a chance to talk." He ripped it into a million little pieces.

When he emerged, finally, after a long, very hot shower, he was surprised to find the house orderly, quiet, and seemingly empty. He helped himself to some orange juice in the glass pitcher in the refrigerator, then took down a bowl and poured some cold cereal into it, the sugary kind he'd liked since he was a kid. When he felt bad, the stuff made him feel better. He was positive that's why little kids liked it too. Parents didn't realize that Sugar Frosted Flakes were a kind of mood elevator. Or maybe they did, and that's why they didn't want to buy the sweet stuff.

Spooning it up and slurping down the milk, he realized he was extremely hungry, so he went to the refrigerator and opened the door to study the contents. Wrapped things in silver foil and covered bowls probably held dinner remains, so he checked out sandwich fixings. He made a large combination platter with turkey, bologna, swiss cheese, ham, lettuce, tomato, and gobs of mayo spread on Italian bread. Two pickles were forked up from a wide-mouthed jar. Just as he was about to bite into his creation, he heard someone behind him. He turned, mouth open, the sandwich raised up. It was his father. He must have been working in his office. Philip never bothered to look for him in there because even if he found his dad, it wouldn't do any good if he was working. The man wouldn't talk to him until he was through, anyway.

He put his sandwich down. This was a set-up, leaving Dad all alone in the house with the bad kid, to get him to have a real heart-to-heart talk. He could hear his mother telling his father to take care of things: "You tell him, you explain to him." How come she still didn't know they never talked to each other? Not really, not

94

meaningfully. Not when anything got decided much more than how much allowance he was going to get for the year or if they should get Rangers and Knicks tickets or just Knicks. Well, he'd just have to go through the motions here. Funny, for almost the first time in his entire life, he wasn't afraid of his father. He felt a kind of kinship with him, as injured party. But he still hadn't figured out why his father had been injured. Had his mother been some kind of damaged goods when they married? Used merchandise? On sale at reduced prices?

"Your mother —" his father began but Philip cut him off.

Through a mouthful of sandwich, he said, "Don't tell me what she thinks. I want to know what you have to say . . . Dad," he added after a slight pause.

"I'm not here on any mission," his father began again. That was better. Philip listened and chewed his food. "Let's get one thing straight. You do not have the right ever to go through someone's private papers. Not mine, not your mother's, not Claire's, not anyone's — ever. Not legally, not morally, not ethically."

"Check," said Philip.

"What you were looking for, I don't know. And I don't care, frankly. This business has gone far enough and I'm serving you notice that this is the end. You're never to do that again."

"Double check," said Philip, still eating, surprisingly hungry.

"You can ask if there's something you want to know." His father pushed away from the table and started to get up.

"That's it?" Philip said. He stopped chewing.

His father nodded.

"But . . . but don't you want to know, I mean, isn't there anything else you have to say?" He had envisioned a cozy talk, the two of them getting down to It, The Subject. How she had betrayed them both. Weren't they going to speak about it?

"Nope," his father said, like Gary Cooper in a western.

95

"But she did it to you too. Unless you knew every-thing and didn't say." Philip thought a moment. Why was his father not picking up on this? "Are you on her side?"

"She's not 'her.' She's your mother. And yes, I am. I'm always on her side. And your side. And Claire's, even when she acts like a jerk. You know, I'm not surprised she's been doing these strange things. Your sister has the capacity to be rebellious and silly. But I didn't think you'd be silly."

"I am not being silly."

"Of course you are. Do you really think I mind that your mother was married before? It was just a college crush, impulsive. I don't hold her past against her. And you shouldn't either, though it must have been tough for you to find out."

"Tough? Find out? Doesn't anyone believe in being honest around here?"

"Why, son? Are you owed an explanation of your mother's past? Or mine, too, for that matter?"

A wave of heat swept over Philip. "Don't tell me that you were married before too."

"Don't panic. That's not what I meant. It's just that you seem to behave as though this information were owed to you, that you have a right to it."

"Well, it was my girlfriend. She knew, and her father, and I felt like a jerk finding out." Suddenly, he realized what was happening. He and his father were having that talk, the talk that they never had. He was being honest and his father was listening. What was going on? All of a sudden everything was upside down. First Claire going punk, then meeting Liz and her father, then what he'd learned about his mother, and now this. Life was weird. Truly.

"I'm sorry," his father said, as if he really did mean it. "You shouldn't have had to find out that way. Maybe you should have been told long ago. I don't know. It was up to your mother to tell you her own way, in her own good time."

"No. Now. She should have told me *now*, and not let me feel like a jerk."

"Take it up with her," his father said, getting up and moving toward the door.

"She'll have to get in line," Philip said, looking down at the remains of his sandwich. He imagined his mother standing at the end of a line, behind Liz, Kenneth, Claire. But not his father. Maybe they'd squared a few things away. His dad was not the enemy. He wasn't such a bad dad, even though he never called him Phil. "Say, Dad," Philip said. "Could you sometimes call me Phil, and not just Philip all the time like I was in school?"

"Sure," his father said. "All you had to do was ask." He walked out of the kitchen.

Philip picked up his sandwich. Maybe it would be okay going to those Knick games together. Have a few hot dogs, some peanuts. They could talk during halftime, maybe get a few more things straight. The thought wasn't unpleasant at all.

Philip's problem, as one day after another passed, was that not talking to people you were mad at didn't help make your anger better. In fact, it made it worse. He didn't know which was harder: ignoring his mother or walking stiffly past Liz. At first, Liz tried to call him, or to approach him in the hall before class or in the cafeteria. The feeling Philip got as he turned away from her was delicious and satisfying. *Now she'll see how it feels,* he said to himself. *Let her be the one who's hurt.* He didn't really care that his father and her dad had tried to get him to understand. Why should he be the understanding one? Let them come to him. But when Liz came to him, he turned his back.

After a while, she stopped trying. His mother did too. She'd gotten the message after several mornings at breakfast when he scarcely spoke to her, and several evenings when he avoided dinner, having stuffed himself at McDonald's before returning home. No way was he going to suffer anymore. They would have to pay.

But suffering, he discovered, was a cold and lonely occupation. When you did it, you did it alone. Gareth wasn't really interested in all the ins and outs of his mother's past and Liz's father's incredible participation. He wanted to talk about the sensational new girl he'd met who was, could Philip believe this, amazingly tall *and* gorgeous, "a veritable Jerry Hall to my Jagger," Gareth exulted. Philip didn't bother to point out that Mick Jagger was but a few heads high compared to Gareth. He didn't bother to act interested. After a while, Gareth complained to Philip that he was "goddamn boring" and started telling his other friends all about Rhonda.

And it was only a very small satisfaction that he and his father got along better. Seeming to understand Philip's mood, his father made no further overtures to him about talking to his mother, or apologizing. It amazed Philip how well his father understood how he was feeling. One night, in fact, just as he was going to sleep, a revelation hit him hard, like a smack on his head, and he sat bolt upright in bed. His father knew because *he'd* had his own problem understanding when his mom had told him! Of course, that was it. They both had to cope with this news.

The next morning he awoke feeling a comradeship with his father. He resolved to get over all his bad feelings as his dad had done and get on with his life. Just as he pulled his sweatshirt over his head and raked his fingers through his hair before going to breakfast, his door pushed open and Claire stood on the threshold. She'd changed her punk hairstyle for something close to her old style and, for once, her school uniform hung to her knees instead of being hiked up high to expose tattered tights split with a dozen runs. This was, for the first time in a long while, someone who resembled the old Claire, his sister.

He hadn't answered her note and had ignored her presence for the last week, too, though it wasn't hard to do as she spent very little time at home anyway. Still, the first thing she said was, "You didn't answer my note."

"Not necessary." He didn't want to give her the time of day.

"You're acting like a real creep. Mom —"

"I don't think you have the right to tell me I'm acting creepy to anyone, not after what you've pulled!"

Claire didn't answer him, but she stared at him furiously.

"I have the right to my feelings, you know," he blurted out. "You're not the only one, big shot. You're just jealous because it's not only your rebellion they care about anymore. Now they want to know how I'm feeling."

"Oh, drop it, asshole," Claire said. "Who wants to see you acting like I did? Some of the stuff I've done isn't so admirable."

"But it gets their attention, doesn't it?"

"Who's this 'they'? You mean Mom and Dad? Hey, you can get their attention any time you want. Just talk to them."

"This is a riot, coming from you, Queen Claire."

She flushed. "I know it sounds ridiculous but maybe by acting the way I did I learned that all I had to do was state my case. And maybe compromise."

"So you're not going to California?"

She smiled. "Yes, I can apply. But the deal is if my SATs are too low and my grades go down, the application's withdrawn."

"I get it, blackmail them!"

"Look, no one asked you to get involved. No one asked you to go through people's stuff or anything."

Philip began to get very angry. Claire, too, mouthing the party line? "I don't see where you come off getting involved in this. Besides, the pictures were right out in the open, anyone could have found them, in the cabinet in the living room."

"So you saw the yearbook. Yeah, well, Mom was a little dense about that. She kept saying she was going to tell you —"

"And you knew all along, right?"

"Yeah, right, when I was born, Mom said, 'Hey,

Claire, I want to tell you about this guy I was married to before.' No, dumbbell, I found out a couple of years ago."

"And you knew all along who Liz was."

"No . . . honest, I didn't. Really, Phil," she grabbed his arm. "I had no idea. I just knew there'd been this college marriage. Maybe Mom talked to me about it because she was afraid with my seeing boys and everything that I'd do something impulsive as she had, with this guy, and it had turned out badly for her. It isn't exactly something she's proud of, you know."

"But you knew . . . you were with Liz that day. You had to know!"

"No," she went on. "Liz found me. I was out on the street, wandering the West Side, feeling so cruddy because I couldn't get a hearing anywhere — not at home, not at school — and my book was going terrible. I was blocked —"

"Claire, you are so full of melodramatic bullshit. Christ, I'm going to be late for school!"

"So I didn't know until Liz's dad told me that day. But kid, you have to hear this . . . it made it easier for me to talk to her, to them. To tell them what I really wanted. Because it sort of laid them open, you see, to have you find out like this, by accident. They're not gods, you know. They're human, they're people. They make mistakes and everything. It sort of all comes into focus. Then you can admit you make mistakes, and everybody gets on with their business. It's really a lot like life."

"It is life," Philip said, his voice dull. He didn't want to go to school anymore. He felt drained.

"And you're making a big mistake blaming Liz. She's really terrific. She wasn't hiding anything from you. She didn't think it mattered. And her mother, and our mom, they're two different people."

"But we could have been . . ." He couldn't say it.

"This is not incest, Philip. Don't give me that Greek tragedy crap. I've had enough of that in school this year. We are not Electra and Oedipus and all those other unhappy Mediterraneans. We're just some kids on the

100

Upper East Side who can't seem to get anything straight."
She put her hands on his shoulders. "Right?"

He wrestled away from her.

"Okay, buddy-boy, suit yourself. I'm getting something to eat. You want to crawl in a hole and die, do it on
your own time. But you're missing a chance to make
something here, this connection. And believe me, lucky
you, you'll be getting something it took me years longer to
find."

"Yeah, what's that? My own way?"

"No, stupid. Parents."

CHAPTER FOURTEEN

Philip cut school that day. He got on the subway, took it down two stops, and got off. He was upset, angry, and teary, and he knew he couldn't face classes, work, his friends, the cafeteria, Liz. Maybe especially Liz. He didn't know if he had really loved her but now he got a sick feeling whenever he thought of her.

He hadn't been real up-front with Claire, and she had tried to be with him. They had never had a talk like that, especially not about their parents. And he knew she had opened up. Yet he couldn't. She'd always gotten along great with their dad. How could he tell her what he was most ashamed of was having wanted this other man to be his father, then finding out *he might have been?* It was scary, almost like wishing someone was sick and then finding out that they had gotten sick. You were responsible. He felt as if he'd personally invented this first marriage to suit his fantasy. The thought was more than scary; it was perverse. *Then it must make me a pervert,* he thought. *A perverted guy. A real sicko.*

With his backpack slung over one shoulder he walked street after street, trying to find some handle on everything.

After a while, he found himself on Lexington Avenue, near the bookshop-gallery where his mother worked. Since she was exactly the person he didn't want to see, he wondered how it had happened. Did his feet just play a trick on him, carrying him off somewhere he never intended to go? Or had it been that he was just thinking so hard he wasn't paying attention to things like street numbers?

At her corner he hesitated before crossing. Maybe he would just pass by casually and peek in the window. Sometimes his mom would be putting away some books she'd just been showing a customer, climbing a curved wooden ladder and lifting incredibly heavy volumes up onto the high shelves. Heavy *old* volumes. It struck him then, hard, that she was just like Kenneth — like Liz's dad, her ex-husband. They liked the past, the two of them. Different pasts, sure, but stuff from way back in time. And yet they were all stuck in this messy present, trying to go back in their heads to what they probably thought was a better time. His mom was hung up on the Renaissance, Italian things, Kenneth on early man, maybe millions of years separating them, right? He wasn't sure. Billions, it could be.

Through the dusty window cluttered with volumes of art history he could see her desk, near the front. The chair was empty but draped over the back was a jacket from one of his mother's "work suits."

A hand grabbed his shoulder. He jumped, then turned around. It was Mr. Levy, the store's owner, an old guy with a neatly cropped white beard and a thatch of thick, white, curly, Santa Claus hair. Mr. Levy grinned at him and kept his hand on Philip's shoulder.

"Zo," he said in his gruff, accented English. "It's a zgool holiday, I zee."

"Yes, Mr. Levy . . . I mean, no it isn't . . . I mean, I didn't go today but —"

Mr. Levy smiled and nodded. Somewhere in his old eyes Philip could see that funny light that grown-ups sometimes got which meant, *Yeah, I know what you're up to. I did the same thing once.* Everyone was into history, Philip guessed, doing the same things again and again. Repeating, like a broken record.

103

Mr. Levy took his hand off Philip's shoulder. "Don't be zuch a ztranger no more," he said. After years and years in America, Mr. Levy retained all his Old World manner and accent. Philip's mom often commented on how much this seemed to help his business, selling valuable old books and prints. "It gives the shop cachet, an authenticity," she told Philip's father. "And makes me think that when he goes home at night, the accent goes bye-bye. I've occasionally caught him in unaccented conversations when he's alone in his office."

Philip liked his mother's descriptions of Mr. Levy, who now bowed in courtly style to Philip and entered his front door. He also liked the fact that Mr. Levy did not snoop, did not ask why he had come or whether he wanted to come in and see his mother. He wondered, briefly, what kind of father Mr. Levy had been to his now-grown children. Did he not snoop on them, or had he been a hateful tyrant whose kids thought he was only kind to customers? Philip felt he wouldn't have made this distinction until recently, until he himself had discovered that things were not always as they seemed. Sighing, he pulled open the door to the shop and, without thinking about it, walked in and saw his mother.

She was standing in the back, helping someone find something on a low shelf. Bent gracefully, her back to him, she gestured with one hand as she used the other to steady herself as she moved down the row of books. Finding what she was looking for, she drew it out of the shelf and handed it tenderly to the tall, thin man standing nearby. Then she moved around and glanced toward the front. When she saw Philip, she smiled eagerly, then that smile faded as she walked toward him. She was realizing that he was not in school. She looked at her watch: 11:30 A.M. Now he was in for it. Why had he come?

"Why are you here?" she said, as if reading his mind. But her sternness was mixed with concern. "Are you all right? Are you ill?" She put the back of her hand up, to check his forehead. He shook his head away.

"I don't know why I came to see you. I guess it's because we have to talk. Dad wants me to apologize, I know. So does Claire. But I think you have to apologize to me too. So I didn't go to classes."

"You could have talked to me at home, Phil."

"No." He was adamant. "No, we had to be away. By ourselves. I don't like to talk about this there." Now that sounded pompous to him. Judgmental. He was sort of sorry he'd said it.

She looked hurt. He could see how unhappy she'd been these last days. The strain showed in her face, which was kind of pale and puffy. But she recovered and became more the businesslike Mom he was used to. "All right, we'll go somewhere. I'll tell Mr. Levy." She went off to find her boss. It was always strange coming into the shop; he didn't do it very often. Claire liked the place and last year had hung out there often, looking at different books and prints. Philip had thought this strange until he had realized she was trying to meet boys there; his mother used to talk about the college kids and the graduate students who came in. Had his mother's store provided Claire with her entrée into the world of the punks? It was a strange notion but not impossible. There were punky kids who liked putting references to classical music and art in their poems or songs, in their clothes and jewelry. They used everything.

His mother returned, wearing her jacket, and he left the shop with her, pushing open the door and holding it for her the way he'd been taught. He realized as they walked outside together that this was one of those rare times when they met that they hadn't hugged and kissed. She hadn't even tried, except to put her hand near his forehead. Was that part of their relationship finished from now on? She couldn't give him a kiss, or he wouldn't let her? And what on earth was he going to say to her once they were alone at lunch, in some restaurant, with only the waiter and busboy nearby to hear their conversation? He felt that his behavior said it all.

The place they went to was in the front of a hotel, a newly renovated cafe with small tables and a strange menu with lots of light stuff he didn't care for: cheese plates and fruit, cold poached fish, watercress and endive. "No hamburgers?" he asked the waitress. His mother suggested the roast beef sandwich on a brioche. He shook his head. He ended up ordering what he didn't want, cold pasta. He felt he was making a statement. "But you don't even like cold pasta," his mother reminded him. He shook his head nobly. He would take his punishment like a man. She ordered a vegetable platter with sesame sauce. "You can have some of mine," she said as if she'd asked for a Big Mac with fries — something he'd want. He didn't want anything from her anymore. Yes he did. He wanted her to say she was sorry, that it was a terrible mistake, that she'd been wrong but no, they'd never been married. It was all a big lie. He wanted things back the way they'd been before, his sister bossy and sure of herself, his father silent and removed, his mother always there for him. He was uncomfortable with change. But maybe they all were.

It was his mother who started the conversation.

"This must be very hard for you," she said.

He didn't reply.

"But if you're going to do something as foolish as miss school and jeopardize your future, your work, and your grades, then we'd better get everything straight right now. And I do not approve of your cutting classes for any reason, I want you to know that."

Ha. She didn't approve. Well, I don't approve of what she did, either.

His mother put her hand on his arm and though he tried to move away she closed her fingers on his skin. Her hand was cold. "I'm sorry this has caused you pain. It's unbelievable that you would have met his daughter, out of all the young girls in the world, but that doesn't change the fact that I was indeed married before your father, however briefly. That I did love someone else. And we did live together. Is it such a big deal? You have many friends whose parents were divorced, then remarried. Some even more than once. Why is it so hard for you to accept this about me?"

Philip shrugged. There was a great lump in his chest, a burning, hard lump like a piece of coal in a grill, glowing fiercely. The lump made it hard to speak. He loved his mother so much. She had gone and ruined it.

"I know it's because you met her . . . Liz. His daughter. But your relationship can go on. No, I mean it, Phil. You have to be grown up about this, otherwise it's going to ruin things for you in the future with any girl. People have pasts, they've done things they may not like, sometimes terrible things. Then when their children find out, they have to live through them again. Maybe there are experiences that we have that are not supposed to be *published*.

"This happened to me, I know you won't believe it, but I'm going to tell you a story now, about your grandma. You must never let on you know when you see her because it would hurt her a great deal. But when I was close to your age, maybe older, I think I was sixteen, I had to get a copy of my birth certificate. I needed a Social Security number, and to get a card you had to show your proof of age and date of birth. My mother wanted to send it in herself but I was being independent, getting a summer job. I think it must have been at a summer camp. So I made a huge fuss about doing it myself and she gave me a copy. Well, I read it before I put it in the envelope, and one part asked how many children were born before this child. In that space it said three. I was terribly shocked. Three children? You know I have only my older brother, your uncle Larry."

His mother's eyes had gotten full, wet, as she told Philip the story, as if she was reliving this moment and always would. She took a deep breath. "I had no idea what this meant, so I charged in and confronted her. She had this secret she didn't want me to know: that she had had two babies who had been born and then died right away. One had a terrible birth defect, something wrong with the heart, the other hadn't developed right, she wouldn't even tell me. The doctors didn't want her to have any more. They told her she would kill herself with another

107

pregnancy. But she wanted another child, she wanted me, a daughter, so badly. So she did it anyway. She risked her health and she risked my health and I could have been born with something horribly wrong. They didn't know why this happened; they couldn't test for it, and it was a very, very long shot that it would be normal, for me and for her."

She paused, cleared her throat, then waited as the food was put in front of them. They both stared at the plates they did not want. Then she said, "I was not kind to my mother. I was like you. I went on a tear. I lashed out at her, not for risking her life, for trying to have a child she wanted desperately, but for not telling me, for letting me find out so cruelly, to see it on my birth certificate. Did she think she was going to keep it a secret forever? Two whole children born, my brother and sister, and she was going to drop the whole thing? I was devastated. She didn't know what to say. I think we didn't speak for a few days. I suppose we forgave each other but I don't know how. Some terrible things were said, mainly by me. And I made a vow that I would never do that to my child, never let them find something like that out. You can see, of course, where that promise got me." She smiled a little quick smile, the corners of her mouth turning up in a little grimace of regret.

"So now the wheel turns around again. And here we are." She picked up her fork and began to push her vegetables around on her plate. "Are we going to say terrible things to each other? And then one day will you have this conversation with your son or daughter, and tell them what happened with your mother?" She gulped, hard, as if swallowing down her memories, her painful story, then she put down her fork and began to cry very softly. The tears in her eyes spilled over down her cheeks and she picked up her napkin and began to dab at her face clumsily.

"I'm sorry, Mom," Philip began automatically. He hated it when she cried. She almost never cried and he hated being the one to make her. Except it wasn't his fault, really, it was this story she told him, her own past confronting her. But what was anyone supposed to do with all this information? Lock it up in a vault and throw away the key? The past was such a dangerous place; how could anyone feel comfortable there? And his mother did, because she loved to study it, loved things that were old. And Kenneth, he loved it too. Trouble was, though, that no one wanted to live in their own pasts. They wanted to create different ones for themselves. Even he did, with a different father. He had tried to make it be Kenneth.

"Mom, I want to tell you something. I . . . with Dad . . . I never felt we got along like a father should with a son. And when I met Kenneth, he was so much like someone I wanted to know. I just wanted it to be him," he said in a rush. She was still wiping at all those tears. "Aw, gee, Mom, you don't have to cry. I don't really feel that way anymore. Jeez, Mom, Dad and I are getting along a whole lot better ever since all this happened."

She nodded. "I knew you would feel that way about Ken."

Ken. She called him Ken. The lump started to burn again.

"That's why I was so afraid for you — not that you would discover my secret, nothing soap-operaish, that wouldn't have bothered me. But Ken is someone about whom there is such an aura of romance, the romance of his occupation, of his craziness, his own excitement about life. It's very seductive. What a tragedy that he lost Vera, his second wife. She was so much of what he really wanted and needed. I doubt he'll ever marry again. She was my old roommate from college . . ."

"She was?" This, too, was amazing. Liz's father divorced his mother and married her roommate? Her friend?

His mother's eyes took on a funny glow as she remembered. "I used to tell her all about him. She was the one who encouraged me to marry him so young. She must have adored him from afar, listening to all my stories, watching the two of us together. She should have been the one from the start; she was so much more right. A good sport, a really game lady. And as it turned out, that

was why she died so young — because she was an adven-
turer, because she was so bloody devoted to him, heart
and soul. She would go anywhere. But maybe that
wouldn't have happened. It's always an accident, isn't it?
Fate? She was bitten by a mosquito, that's all. But this
mosquito was carrying something awful, a form of en-
cephalitis. She died in a week. She was a fine person."

"How do you know all this?" Philip asked. It was as
if he were listening to the story line of a movie, not something people he knew had lived through. This was fantastic, unbelievably tragic. Did Liz know all this? Suddenly,
he wanted to see her, right away.

"Ken wrote to me. We still kept in touch. After all,
he'd married my best friend, with a little interference
from me. I made sure he knew all her good points, believe
me. He needed her. And they had been very happy, much
happier than I ever would have been. Your mom is really
just a stay-at-home kind of person. But after Vera died, we
wrote less and less. Men don't really write letters and
keep up friendships the way women do. So we had lost
touch. And then it seemed so hard to pick up the thread,
after I realized he was back in New York. I'm sure he felt
the same way. With the two of you involved, it would
have been very strange. Plus, of course, he's a gentleman.
And perhaps he thought your dad would have minded. I
don't know. We don't speak. That part of my life is over.
No regrets."

"Uh, Mom, would it be okay if I went back to school
now?"

"Of course, Philip. I can give you a note about this
morning if you want to be covered officially. I don't
mind. But why don't you eat some roast beef first?
Okay?" she asked, meaning is everything okay now, with
us? She gestured to the waitress and ordered Philip the
meat sandwich he'd really wanted in the first place.

He took a huge bite of roast beef. Suddenly, he was
enormously hungry, as if he hadn't eaten in days. He
looked at his mother and he nodded, chewing furiously.
It was more than okay. It was fine.

CHAPTER FIFTEEN

OF COURSE EVERYTHING WAS GOING TO END UP LIKE IN THE MOVies, Philip fantasized as he took the subway down to school. He would find Liz, make her sit down and listen to him, and he would tell her — what? That he forgave her? He wasn't entirely sure what he had to forgive her for. Was information withheld the same as telling a lie, or was it just covering up? It seemed to Philip that if a politician didn't tell something important, he could be removed from office. So it must be just like lying. But he didn't think Liz was a liar; in fact, he thought of her rather tenderly as a kind of victim, just like him. After all, if his mother had stayed married to her father, then her mother would never have ventured into some dangerous place where that mosquito would have bitten her. She'd have been snug and secure, off somewhere in a hotel. But then Liz wouldn't have been born Liz, and he wouldn't have been Philip, either. The two of them would have been combined in a crazy way, like some old statue that was half person-half animal, two parts stuck together helterskelter.

But what happened was no movie. He found her leaving the cafeteria, heading off to her next class, and she wouldn't talk to him. She glared at him, wounded. He was stunned by her anger. All of his plans for reconcilia-

111

111

tion washed away with that one look. Now what was he going to do?

He got a week's detention for cutting morning classes, so by the time he left school that day most of the crowds outside had dissipated. For the first time since this whole mess had surfaced, he felt the need for some distraction, of kids from school jabbering and chattering about stupid things like too much homework in physics or not enough sleep because of some late movie they just had to watch, old stuff, like from the sixties. He wasn't even born in the sixties. The decade was like some twilight god, sleeping, that roused itself occasionally to send out a moment of a dream, an impression, of what it had been like. More past. More living in the past. Everyone he knew seemed to be chasing the past, except him. He wanted something in the present. He wanted to be with Liz.

Then, as if he had conjured her up, there she was on the subway, on his very East-Side Lexington Avenue going-home subway, clutching her schoolbag and a big shopping bag. That was it: she'd gone to buy some clothes after school, oh lucky break. She was smiling and talking to one of her girlfriends, a frizzy-haired stringy type he thought was called Holly. He remembered Gareth making a series of awful puns on her name. Liz was animatedly explaining something to Holly (or maybe that wasn't Holly, maybe that was the girl who was actually named something ordinary like Debbie but who wanted everyone to call her Aretha, like the soul singer). He made his way over to where they were standing and, pretending nothing had happened, gave Liz a big grin and said, "Hi!"

She turned around then turned her back to him in one smart move.

Holly or Debbie-Aretha stared at him, wondering who this person was who deserved to be treated so rudely.

The train made thundering, crashing noises. "Hi, Liz," he practically screamed.

"She isn't interested in talking to you," the friend fi-

112

nally said after Liz did not turn around. "I'm not trying to interfere. It just seems obvious that this does not interest her."

Philip stared at the girl. Liz knew the oddest people.

"Liz," he hollered, and the train screeched to a stop so the cry echoed in the relative silence. She did not move. People shoved past them, rushing to get out the doors. All at once, just as the doors began to close, Liz darted through and left Philip stranded in the subway, standing with the frizzy, stringy girl, staring at the closed doors.

"I could have predicted this," the girl said. "I'm not at all surprised. There's a real statement being made here and I don't think you should ignore what she's saying."

"How do you know what she's saying? She didn't say anything!"

"It's very Zen."

Philip stared at the girl. Sometimes he thought his school was chock-full of extremely strange people vying for first prize in some kind of weird competition. Then he realized that he was probably just one of the weirdos, too, no prize-winner like this girl was, but all the same simply one of the inmates.

The strange girl got off one stop before Philip. He walked home looking everywhere for Liz, hoping that she was so ashamed of her behavior that she was seeking him out.

Back home, alone in his room, he realized that he had blown it. All those chances he'd had, to answer Liz's phone calls, to talk to her at school. He'd been the one to turn his back first. He was a jerk. If you really cared about someone, you had to listen to them. You had to give them a chance. That's what everyone had been trying to tell him — his parents, his sister, even Kenneth. And he did not do this for Liz. So now she would never speak to him again as long as she lived. And they would go to the same school, and even be in class together, and she wouldn't even look at him.

He began to really suffer. He sent her letters. She sent

113

them back. He sent her notes in class. She ripped them up. He sent her flowers. He didn't know what happened to them. He spent his entire allowance on a box of Godiva chocolates, and discovered Gareth and a bunch of his buddies devouring them at lunch. "Hey, want a piece of this stuff? It's really good. Someone sent them to Liz's dad."

It was to Gareth that he confided his suffering, finally. He knew he was wrong, and that it was going to make him look bad. Gareth took it well, though, and was surprisingly sympathetic.

"So you felt it was kind of like incest, huh? I can understand that would be a problem. And you saw her, I mean, Liz's mother, no wait a second, *your* mother, right? In that slide, the night we were at that lecture. I fell asleep during that slide show. Think of what I was missing! Family drama, the human comedy. So you want it all to be okay now? Liz is really pissed at you."

"I sent her the candy."

"What candy? You don't mean the stuff we had in the cafeteria? That expensive stuff? With all the fillings? In the gold box?"

Philip kept nodding and nodding.

"That was you? Boy, you must have felt like a dope. And I ate half that box. Guess I owe you one. Want to try some grass? My father's private source came through. He hides it inside that sculpture over there." Gareth gestured toward a square box with a colored design in lucite on the front. When you pressed a button, the sculpture lit up and displayed various intricate patterns. Grass inside? It didn't surprise Philip. Maybe Gareth's father was a dope dealer after all.

"No thanks. I have enough problems without getting busted."

"You're real paranoid, aren't you? Listen, why don't you just forget about Liz? She's very stubborn. Very, very loyal, but when she's crossed very stubborn. Lots of the best people are that way. Take Monica, this girl I've been seeing. She goes to prep school in Boston. Flies in on the shuttle on her father's credit card. She could be very loyal, but as long as I don't have enough bucks she's going to consider transferring her loyalty, if you see what I mean."

"Actually no," Philip said. "I don't see what this has to do with Liz."

"I'm not supposed to say anything, but . . . she's moving."

Philip's heart began to race, pushing hard against his ribs. "Where? When? Don't tell me they're going to Africa!"

"No, nothing serious as that. But her dad's got an offer to teach in California. Some special chair in his field. Anthropology? Isn't that what he does? Or is it archaeology? I keep getting them mixed up. Pots and pans or people? Anyhow, they have this grant and he's only got a few months left at the museum, so off they go for a year to sunny CA. How's that for news, bud? Hey, don't look at me that way. It's not like it's my fault."

His life was over. That was it. The only girl he'd ever liked and first he finds out they're practically related genetically, then bam, he gets used to the idea and she gets on a plane. Oh, this was Hollywood all right, but it wasn't the movie he'd tuned into. It was the other movie, the soppy one with all the crying at the end, the one he never wanted to watch. The characters part forever, or one of them dies, or they marry other people and then meet and they still love each other but it's too late.

"And Monica has this friend," Gareth was saying. "She's really cool, from Greenwich or somewhere fancy, and she'd love to meet one of my friends and she's not as tall as Monica and would love a date, so how 'bout it next time they shuttle on in?"

Philip was about to tell Gareth that he had no intention of dating, that his heart was permanently broken — for God's sake, how could he even consider such a thing? — when the front door opened and in walked this very large, short, squat man with a huge midsection that pushed out the front of his plain but expensive-looking

115

suit. Philip decided at once that this must be Gareth's father's accountant or stockbroker or personal business manager because the man looked sort of Neanderthal but smart, like lots of those self-made businessmen Philip saw in the pages of his father's business magazines. The pizza kings or the cookie kings or the plastic piece that fits inside the top of the camera or VCR or something that makes them millions.

"Hey, Gareth," the man said in a distinct Brooklyn accent. Very Brooklyn. Or was it the Bronx?

"Hey, Dad," said Gareth.

Dad? This was Dad? The owner of all this incredible high-tech art? The man who bought all this super-modern furniture? The father of this incredibly tall, cool kid with the fuzzy background? The drug smuggler? Where was the elegant West Coast-type Philip had envisioned with the leather jacket and the fancy sunglasses?

"Dad, Phil . . . Phil, Dad."

The man moved over toward Philip and extended his pudgy hand. "How's it goin'?" he said companionably. He must have been an inch shorter than Philip. Five-seven, max. Was Gareth's mother a giraffe? And what on earth did Gareth's father do? Now he could find out.

"Home a little early," Gareth said. He looked relieved, as well he might. A few minutes later and he'd have been caught stealing from his father's stash. His father's stash! This was the man with the stash?

"So, a friend from school?" Gareth's dad said.

"Yeah," said Gareth. "He used to take Liz out. You remember Liz, from boarding school? The girl whose father used to bring the skulls around to talk about?"

"Yeah, yeah," his father said. "The bones."

"Well, get this. His mom used to be married to Liz's dad, except he didn't know it, so he got really pissed that nobody told him, and now he's broken up with Liz and I'm trying to fix him up with a friend of Monica's."

Philip was astounded at this conversation. Gareth was talking to his father as easily as he talked to the kids at school, like they were real pals. What was going on?

116

"Yeah, yeah," his father said. "That Monica is a real doll." He turned to Philip. "So your dad used to be married to someone related to Liz?"

"No, you've got it backwards. His mother and her father."

"What does it matter? You kids have your own crazy ideas about things nowadays. Take me, for instance. I've been married four times. Can you beat that? But my son here, he doesn't mind a bit. As long as we stay together. You like number four, don't you?" he said, turning toward Gareth.

"She doesn't ask me why I don't play basketball. I like that," Gareth said.

"Lucky I run the kind of business that can support all these wives."

Here was his chance. "And what is it you do?" Philip said casually.

"Bras," Gareth's father said. "Get it? I can support these women!"

Gareth made a face. This was, Philip gathered, the old family joke. He pretended to laugh, wondering how he could have been so wrong about anyone. A bra manufacturer. Married four times. Short and fat. Nice, but no CIA agent. Unless he knew nothing about the CIA. But all those mysterious trips? And all this incredible furniture? And art?

"Got to visit my factories in Hong Kong next week," Gareth's father was saying. "Gretchen won't be going, so she'll help you manage. Gretchen is number four," he explained to Philip. "My doll."

Philip looked at Gareth. Gareth was grinning broadly. He was enjoying this, this comedy-drama of Philip meeting his father. He'd encouraged all those romantic notions! He wanted Philip to think it was something dashing, not underwear. His dad was a garmento, four marriages notwithstanding. And Gareth took it as a huge joke.

Philip prepared himself to be furious. It was happening all over again: he was led on, told one story while the

117

truth lay elsewhere, permitted to believe one thing, played the fool. Then he looked over at grinning Gareth. Gareth cocked his head toward his father as if to say, "Isn't this a hoot?" and Philip burst out laughing. Of course it was all a joke — the CIA, the dope dealing, the stash in the sculpture. How could he be angry at anyone? You thought you knew something, you pretended things were one way, then you found out how they really were. It was like you studied for the wrong test, with the wrong book.

And just then Gareth's father reached into his pocket and took out the biggest roll of cash Philip had ever seen in his life, an immense wad, and he peeled off several bills and told Gareth to have fun while he was away on "business." That was what he said, and there was a funny sound to the way he said *business*. Philip wondered if selling bras was just a front, maybe. Is that how he got all that cash? If so, then all those James Bond movies really sold you a crock. Nothing, but nothing, was what it seemed.

Maybe that even included Liz being mad.

CHAPTER SIXTEEN

THE WEIRD PART WAS THAT IT WAS CLAIRE WHO GOT LIZ TO TALK to Philip. Old Claire, who'd never done Philip a serious favor in her life, celebrating her admission to Stanford University, school of her dreams, and she must have been feeling expansive.

"My astonishing turnaround in attitude and grades," Claire said, "made Mom and Dad think I'd be okay on the coast."

"So that's that," Philip replied. He wasn't exactly glad she was getting her way again, but he was enough of a second child to realize that she'd paved the way for him to go to just about any school, geographically, that his heart desired. So he owed her at least a little attention.

"Isn't it just the best? And you can come and visit, promise, any time you want. And it'll be in California, a great place to come. You'll meet all my friends . . . I know Mom and Dad will let you go alone. And," she said with a heavy significance in her voice, "you'll be able to see someone I know really matters to you."

"Who's that?" Philip said. "You?"

"Liz," Claire said.

"Liz is still in my school," Philip replied. But he felt hot all over, and almost faint. He didn't want to hear again that she was leaving, but he wanted to know everything.

"Not for long. She'll be out there by spring. And her dad is going to be teaching in my school. I may even be able to audit his seminar next year — me, a freshman! It's unheard of, but Liz thinks he can pull some strings for me. Can you believe?"

"Glad he's doing someone in our family a favor."

"Oh, grow up, bro. You are such a bore with your injured pride, really. You shut yourself off from some people who could have made a difference in your development."

Two months ago his sister sounded like Annie Lenox and now she talked like Sigmund Freud. What was coming up next? She changed identities like she changed clothes.

"I know she wants to see you," Claire said.

"Sez who?"

"She can't accept that you won't talk to her."

"I won't talk to her? What about her? She ran away from me on the subway last month. Right out the doors . . . she could have really hurt herself. And she left me talking to this really gross friend of hers. That is such bull, Claire-head."

"Suit yourself," she shrugged. "I was just going to invite you over to her house, a little party later tonight, but I guess you don't want to come."

He rolled over and sat up. Clutching a pillow and pressing it against his stomach, he leaned over and put his face very close to Claire's. He could smell her perfume, something very floral. He hated it. "If you're telling me a lie, you're dead. I'll destroy you. I'll show them your manuscript . . . what you wrote about them . . . what you said in public."

"Oh, that. I tore it up," she said. "This is true, Phil. She told me to ask you. She didn't want to call; she doesn't want any more rejection. I think she really, really likes you. But look, she had to come to terms with something too. It's her father, isn't it? And our mother? She's entitled to have some strong feelings."

"I don't know."

120

"But you'll come, right? You only have a few more weeks before she'll be gone. You have to settle this. You can't let it hang anymore."

"Why are you so interested, Claire?"

She smirked. "Oh, I don't know. She's a neat girl. And I really like her dad."

Philip groaned. "Not you too."

"Like mother —" she said with a start. "Gosh, I never thought of that. Am I sick or what?"

"Yes, Claire. I've always told you that you were the sick one in the family."

"So you're coming," she said, ignoring his remark.

"Why don't we bring Mom along?" he said.

"What a great idea!" said Claire. Then she looked at his expression. "You're being sarcastic, you little twerp." She grabbed the pillow and smacked him across the head with all her might. It hurt.

"Okay, okay, I'll go with you, but only if you call Liz and make sure."

"Oh, I'm sure, Philip. I'm sure." And she walked out of his room, immensely pleased with herself.

Liz's little party turned out to be a big party, and it wasn't exactly just for kids. It was a going-away party for her dad and for herself; she invited about twenty friends. The grown-ups took over the living room and adjacent room, their talk almost a roar, their hands clutching glasses of wine, their hands making quick dives toward the spread of cheese and paté and fruit which adorned the dining table.

Wandering through the apartment behind his sister, Philip peered cautiously into these rooms looking for Liz. Actually, he was terrified to see her, afraid she would turn away from him as she had done on the subway. He was also scared to see her dad, afraid of the welter of feelings that his presence aroused, afraid of that illogical yearning his person awakened in Philip. He had wanted to belong to this man in some way, but when their missed connection emerged it panicked him. He'd heard somewhere an old saying about how hard it was when you finally got what you wanted and, boy, was it true. And look what it had done to him and Liz. Instead of getting close and spending time together they had not spoken for nearly two months. Soon she'd be gone, living on another coast, and he'd be back to drifting around with girls who seemed so fluffy compared to her.

"Well, hi there," someone said, and Philip turned around to see the gangly girl from the subway. What was her name?

"Glad to see you're on speaking terms," she continued. "Anthea," she said finally as he stared at her blankly. Where did he get Aretha? He must have confused her with someone. But knowing her name made her no less strange. "I know you're Philip. Liz talks about you a lot."

Suddenly, he was very interested in this Anthea. He let Claire move ahead of him, into the party, and turned his attention to her. "Does she . . ." he said in what he hoped was a sophisticated manner.

Anthea batted her eyes. She was flirting with him! She was moving in on her friend's territory. Girls were amazing that way. They had no scruples about getting right on with it.

"She's real sorry it ended this way," Anthea said, making some kind of coy expression with her mouth. It was really frightful. I have seen the future, Philip thought, and it's girls like this. Yuck.

"I didn't know it had ended," said Philip. "I wouldn't have been invited tonight if it had, would I?"

"You're in for a rude surprise," she said. "Lots of luck. I'll be around if you need me."

That was uninformative, Philip thought, but now what do I do? How can I approach Liz at all? This is just a waste of time and a potential humiliation.

Gareth rushed over to him, trailed by the tallest woman Philip had ever seen, a wildly beautiful giraffe of a girl who looked twenty years old. This must be Monica.

"Here's Monica," Gareth said at once. Then he lowered his voice. "She's only fifteen. I know, I know, she looks much older. She's a model and when they put eyeliner on her she just ages before your eyes. She has teddy bears in her room at home. Can you dig that? Teddies." He raised his voice. "Hey Mon, Monnie, come meet my absolutely best friend Phil. Wouldn't Phil be just great to fix up with your roomie?"

Monica draped herself on Gareth, like he was a lamppost on which you could lean. She was wearing black leather pants and high-heeled shoes, which added two or three inches to her already fantastic height. Where did they grow women like this? In Iowa, with the tall corn? In California? Didn't Gareth say she was from Greenwich? She must have driven them out of their minds in Connecticut.

"Here to say toodle-ooo, right-oh?" Gareth went on, as if this incredibly long person were not draped all over him, like a coat tossed across a shoulder. "Oh, it's a sad day for us all when Lizzie says goodbye. Of course, in all the years I've known her we've said goodbye about five hundred times. Her dad is always schlepping her off somewhere. She's used to it by now, and so are we. She'll be back. And in the meantime, Monnie is going to keep me company, right?"

Then Monica said the only thing Philip heard her say the entire evening. In this absolutely breathy little baby voice, like a six-year-old's, she breathed, "Uh-huh," nodding her head for additional emphasis. Philip decided she was like a dinosaur — large, quite phenomenal, but very small in the brain department. A leaf-eater.

It was while he was contemplating Monica's length for the thousandth time that he saw Liz, out of the corner of his eye. She was making her way toward the kitchen, which seemed to be where the kids were having their own party. It was now or never. He turned his back on Gareth and Monica, who were not into noticing anyone at that moment, and moved over to Liz. Without thinking, he put his arms around her before she had a chance to respond. She stiffened as he hugged her, but he could feel her breathing hard, her heart beating fast as he pressed himself to her. She did not push him away but she did not respond, either. She allowed herself to be hugged. Tolerated it. As he slowly pulled back from her unyielding body and her rigid flesh, he paused and said, very softly, "I loved you, Liz."

"I know," she said.

"It's too bad, what happened. I was just so mixed up, I couldn't handle it. But I'm here. I wanted to come. And I wanted to see you that day in the subway, to tell you I wanted to try it with you again. Now it's too late . . . you're going and I ruined everything." He hung his head, ashamed.

"Shut up, Phil," she said.

"What?" he said. He looked up at her. She was smiling.

"You sound like such a dope. You acted like such a dope. I mean, so what if your mom was married to my dad? I didn't know it was you, or her. I didn't realize anything until my father looked through those slides for the lecture. It was pretty weird, but it wasn't major. It wasn't something that would make me give anything up, like my relationship with you. It wasn't like she was my mother *and* your mother. I guess I was more surprised by everything than shocked. But you won't talk to me. Claire tells me you're having this enormous temper tantrum."

"She's no one to talk about tantrums."

"Claire is great. She works things out for herself. We're going to be in California together."

"Suit yourself. You can have her instead of me." He started to walk away. She was making him feel like a fool.

"JUST WAIT," Liz hollered. The whole room stopped talking, eating, drinking, dancing. Heads poked out through the kitchen door. Everyone was staring at them.

He looked around. People were waiting for something to happen. Liz was watching him. He wanted to prompt her, to make her say something, but then he just announced it, out loud. "My mom and her dad used to be married. Okay?"

No one said anything.

"Okay," Philip said. "I was the last to find out. So I got mad. I'm not so mad anymore. I'm sorry I acted dumb."

"It's okay," Gareth called out. "We forgive you."

Everyone began to call out things: "We forgive you . . . Who cares? . . . It's okay with us . . . Kiss and make up." All kinds of silly stuff. And then Liz ran up to him and threw her arms around his neck and she was hugging him, tightly, and everything was right again, finally.

He made Liz laugh a lot, later, when they were alone and wrapped around each other and talking about everything that had happened. He told her about his experiences with Gareth and how, when he finally met Gareth's father, it had been such a strange revelation that he was not a slick, cool man of the world but just a really ordinary guy with tons of money.

"But money's romantic, isn't it?" Liz said. "I mean, romantic in a way. You can buy things with it . . . romantic adventures. Right?"

"I think I found out that one person's romantic adventure is another person's nightmare," Philip said. "Why do you have to move to California?"

"It's just for a year. I'll be able to come back to school. And you'll see me 'cause Claire says she's going to bring you out to school with her, in August, when she gets set up. Maybe you can spend a week or two with us. I know my dad would like that. He really likes you a lot."

"He does? Even after all this mess?"

"He never notices. He's not real big on things like emotional problems. I know he seems like a lot of fun, and we're very close and everything, but he kind of lets me down in certain areas. If I'm feeling unhappy or sad or I'm having a problem with a friend he'll listen, but then he'll forget what I'm saying. So by the end of the conversation it's like, 'You'll be okay, right? Now what was it that was bothering you?' "

Philip thought, *At least my father remembers what I'm talking about, even though he isn't the easiest parent in the world to talk to.* "I guess they're really not perfect, none of them," he said.

"I know this is going to sound strange," Liz said, "but I feel jealous of your mother, and it's not just because she was married to my dad first."

"Why my mom?"

"I think it's because what my father remembers about her best is that she was so independent. She did what she wanted to do. My mother seems to have been very hung up on pleasing my father, putting him first. I'm not sure I really like that. It's hard to admit, with her gone, but she's not my role model."

The idea that Philip's mother was a good role model amused him. He wanted to tell Liz about those silent mornings at the breakfast table, and how his mother always played up to their father. But then it struck him that his mother was a kind of link between himself and Liz. A good link, Liz was saying.

Before they could go on discussing this shared cast of characters they started to laugh, then kiss, then moan over the excruciatingly long twelve months of separation that faced them.

"We'll write and talk on the phone, and you could come to California for Thanksgiving," Liz said.

"No, you could come to New York, with Claire, to our house," Philip said.

"I'd have to bring my dad."

Her dad. In Philip's house. "My mom and your dad," he said. It was funny how the idea no longer seemed strange. There was something oddly natural about it — smooth. He couldn't really remember why he'd gotten so upset. Maybe it had to do with being in ninth grade, and falling in love, so he decided to forget about it all and go back to kissing Liz, which was much more fun than thinking about the past.

"BRAAAAAAAAAAAAAAAAAAAAAA!"

A deafening noise filled the apartment. Dr. Cooke was blowing his horn again.